THE
ASSIGNATION

Other Books by Joyce Carol Oates

THE
ASSIGNATION

Stories by
Joyce Carol Oates

THE ECCO PRESS
NEW YORK

THE ECCO PRESS
100 West Broad Street
Hopewell, New Jersey 08525

Published simultaneously in Canada by
Penguin Books Canada, Ltd., Ontario
Printed in the United States of America

Library of Congress Cataloging-in-Publication Data
Oates, Joyce Carol, 1938–
The assignation
A collection of short stories.
I. Title
PS3565.A8A885   1988   813'.54   88-3708
ISBN 0-88001-200-5
ISBN 0-88001-440-7 (paperback)

Designed by Beth Tondreau Design
The text of this book is set in Times Roman

9 8 7 6 5 4 3 2 1

FIRST ECCO PAPERBACK EDITION

Acknowledgments

A number of these narratives have appeared in magazines and journals, often in earlier versions. To the editors of these publications, all acknowledgments and thanks are due.

"Two Doors," "The Quarrel," "One Flesh," "Anecdote," and "Train," in *Exile* (Toronto); "The Boy," in *Playgirl;* "Sharpshooting," in *The Boston Globe Magazine;* "Slow" and "Tick," in *Southern California Anthology;* "Photographer's Model," in *Confrontation;* "Accident" and "Only Son," in *Nit & Wit* (Chicago); "Party" and "Mule," in *Boston Review;* "A Touch of the Flu," "In Traction," and "Heartland," in *Fiction Network;* "Holiday," in *Nit & Wit;* "Eleuthéria" and "Secret," in *Fiction International;* "The Abduction," in *Seventeen;* "Romance," in *Threepenny Review;* "Pinch," in *American Voice;* "Ace," in *New England Quarterly;* "Maximum Security," in *New Directions;* "Fin de Siècle," in *Interview;* "Shelter," PEN/NEA fiction competition winner; "Adultress," in *New Woman;* "Superstitious," in *Bennington Review;* "A Sentimental Encounter," in *Epoch;* "Señorita," in *Northwest Review;* "Desire," in *For Nelson Mandela* (Seaver Books/Henry Holt, 1987); "The Others," in *Twilight Zone;* "Secret Observations on the Goat-Girl," in *Pequod;* "Visitation Rights," in *TriQuarterly;* "The Stadium," in *Omni;* "The Bystander" in *Queen's Quarterly;* "Stroke," "Face," and "August Evening," in *Malahat;* "Picnic," in *High Plains Literary Review;* "The Assignation," in *Antaeus.* "Blue-Bearded Lover" appeared as a special limited edition published by William B. Ewert (Concord, New Hampshire, 1988).

—FOR RUSSELL BANKS

Contents

It is not the voice that commands the story: it is the ear.
    —Italo Calvino, Invisible Cities

THE
ASSIGNATION

One Flesh

They are sitting at opposite ends of the old horsehair sofa waiting for something to happen. A rainy summer night, or is it a rainy autumn night, smelling of wet leaves. A muffled reedy music permeates the room like remembered music in which rhythm is blurred. One by one enormous soft-winged insects fly toward them, or scuttle above their heads on the ceiling. Several clocks tick in unison, sounding like a single clock.

Slow

The wrong time for him to be returning home so she stands at an upstairs window watching as he drives up the driveway but continues a little beyond the area where they usually park in front of the garage and stops the car back by the scrubby evergreen hedge and then there's another wrong thing, it's that she doesn't hear the car door slam, she listens but she doesn't hear, so she turns slow and wondering from the window goes downstairs and at the door where there's still time for her to be hearing his footsteps she doesn't hear them so like a sleepwalker she continues outside moving slowly as if pushing through an element dense and resistant but transparent like water and at the end of the walk she sees that he is still in the car still behind the wheel though the motor has been turned off and the next wrong thing of course is that he's leaning forward with his arms around the wheel and his head on his arms, his shoulders are shaking and she sees that he is crying . . . he is in fact sobbing . . . and in that instant she knows that their life will be split in two though she doesn't, as she makes her slow way to him, know how, or why.

The Boy

There was this boy named Kit, all semester he pestered me with love, called out Hey good-lookin' on the street, after class he'd hang around eyeing me, Hey teach you're a peach, smart aleck giggly staring, wet brown eyes, smooth downy peach-skin didn't look fourteen but he said he was seventeen which might have been true. I said, All right damn you, I drove us to this place I knew in the woods, a motel meant to look like a hunting lodge, fake logs with fake knotholes, I brought two six-packs along, the room smelled of damp and old bedclothes, somebody's hair oil or maybe Airwick, bedspread that hadn't been changed in a long time. It's my strategy to praise, actually I mean everything I say, God I wanted him to feel good, there was some fooling around, getting high, quick wisecracks you roar your head off at but can't remember five minutes later, we were both getting excited, Hey let's dance, we got high and fell across the bed tangling and tickling. I opened his pants and took hold of him but he was soft, breathing fast and shallow, was he afraid? but why? of *me?* hey why? I blew in his ear and got him giggling, I teased and said, O.K. kid now's your chance, Mommy ain't anywhere near, kissed and tickled and rubbed against him, God I was hot, down the hall a radio or TV going loud and then a door slammed and you couldn't hear it, now I was flying high and spinning going fast around a turn in the mountains, Oooooo, hair streaming out behind me like it hasn't done in fifteen years, I was crying no I was laughing, wanted to get him hard damn it, big and inside me like a man, then I'd tell him how great he was, how fantastic, it would make me happy too, not just strung out, part-time shitty teaching jobs that I had to drive twenty-three miles one way to get to, thirty miles the other and just one-year contracts, sorry that's how it is that's how it is all over these days. And these pouches under my eyes and a twisty look that scares the nice shy kids. But he never did get hard, it felt like something little that's been skinned, naked and velvety like a baby rabbit, he was squirming like I'd hurt him or he was afraid I might hurt him, finally he said, I guess I don't love you, I guess I want to go home, but I didn't even hear it, I was thinking Oh fuck it the beer's going to get warm, I closed my eyes seeing the road tilt and spin and something about the sky, filmy little clouds that knock your heart out they're so beautiful. Hey let's dance, kid, I said giggling, let's knock the shit out of this room, he was laughing, maybe he was crying and his nose was running, I just lay there thinking, All right, kid, all right you bastards, this is it.

Sharpshooting

Amid the debris in the garage she'd inherited was an old English bicycle, three-speed, rust-flecked, with a soiled sheepskin seat cover unevenly nibbled by mice. She took it to a bicycle shop and had it spruced up and now in the late afternoons when heat quivers visibly in the air she rides the bicycle in any direction that draws her.

The street on which she lives continues out into the country and changes its character with distance. Concrete yields to sticky black-top yields to gravel that tosses up pebbles and chips and rouses dust in her wake. The proper little aluminum-sided houses with their mowed lawns give way to houses in need of painting and repair, shanties with tin roofs, trailers perched atop cement blocks. There are yards choked with weeds where horses and goats graze and beyond the city limit the road which is now a narrow thinly graveled lane comes to a dead end at the county dump.

Mid-summer afternoons the dump is usually deserted but today there are four or five boys target-practicing with air rifles, they've bicycled out also and she pedals in their direction though the sound of shooting and the *ping!* as pellets hit metal or glass can be jarring to the nerves. Anselm speaks in her ear, *One believes in order to understand,* and she's thinking that in her short candy-striped shorts and her boxy hunter-green shirt she'd make a spectacular moving target outlined against mounds of stationary debris. Old enough to be their mother but boys that age can't judge and can't be relied upon to care.

She straddles her bicycle to watch. Shades her eyes, smiling. A quiet day at the dump except for the boys' rowdy shouts and the repeated *ping! ping! ping!* of the air rifles. She counts four boys, only three rifles. One of the rifles is shared by two curly-haired boys who resemble each other so closely they are surely brothers, or twins.

Today she is wearing a straw hat with a tie under the chin, a red-ribbon tie that matches her lipstick. Rotten straw sandals and painted toenails and when a colleague once asked Why do you paint your toenails but not your fingernails her comeback was, "Because I can't bite my toenails."

Wit, the mother of wisdom.

"Hello," she calls out to the boys. "Are you sharpshooters?"

They're watching her as a little awkwardly—it's tough getting started in this sandy soil—she bicycles closer, straw hat pushed to the back of her head. The boys are between twelve and fourteen years old she would estimate and there's no doubt who the leader is—the tallest, huskiest, a straw-haired boy who stands with his rifle loose in the crook of his arm, watching her with blank startled eyes. She sees there is a quick flash, a connection between them, however, and it is he whom she addresses. "What are you shooting?" she asks.

He mumbles something she can't hear and the boys edge away not exactly rudely but they're embarrassed, they don't want her around, she cups a hand to her ear and says, "Say that again, please?" and the straw-haired boy mumbles again this time a little louder, over his shoulder, "—Just some things."

"Are those real rifles?" she asks. "Are those twenty-twos?"

The boys call back something that sounds like "Nah." She knows the rifles are only air rifles of course but why not flatter the kids.

They're self-conscious because of her, maybe a little excited. Regrouping a short distance away and shooting their rifles giggling among themselves and *ping!* go the guns *ping! ping!* and she covers her ears playfully and straddles her bicycle to watch. It's hot, sticky hot, heat waves squirmy as brain waves, sun like a mad white eye, what remedy but sharpshooting? Tin cans, bottles, plastic milk containers, the remains of mirrors and lamps and kiddies' toys and sofas, chairs, mattresses, kitchen tables, refrigerators, stoves . . . newspapers in bundles and newspapers blown loose, everything at rest, glinting and winking in the sun. It's a place of peace except the boys go wild suddenly as a large rat appears and they run shrieking after it firing their guns.

No luck.

What a racket.

Disappointed, the boys stomp around for a while in the debris, lifting things and tossing them down, smashing things that will smash, swearing loudly in their little-boy voices. When they quiet down a bit she says, "Are there lots of rats out here? They could be dangerous couldn't they? Something that size?"

She wonders does she sound like a mother, when she isn't.

The straw-haired boy, who has been watching her slantwise, suspiciously, says, "Nah—we get 'em all the time out here."

"Are they hard to get?"

"Yeh, they're fast. You saw him."

She says with a little laugh, "*I've* never shot a rifle in my life—a rifle or a gun in my entire life!"

Her tone is wistful but it's just a pose, a voice-intonation. Teaching, you acquire such tricks.

Suddenly the straw-haired boy whirls and raises his rifle and fires at something atop a mound of debris and it appears to be a bird—a redwing or a starling—not a grackle, she'd have recognized, in silhouette, the long flaring tail—that flutters wildly up into the air but manages to fly away. Another boy shoots at it but misses and she calls out, chiding, "*That* wasn't nice! This is 'Be Kind to Birds Week' throughout the state!"

The boys snicker in response, she guesses they are really competing for her attention.

She follows them around still straddling the bicycle since she doesn't think the kickstand will hold in the sand and she doesn't want to lay the bicycle down flat as the boys have done with theirs, she's afraid of the chain getting dirty, the finely calibrated brake apparatus misaligned. When she brought the bicycle to the shop the man said, "Where'd you find *this*?"—meaning it was an old model. Whether his question indicated respect or subtle contempt she didn't know.

It was John Calvin who observed that each man's mind is like a labyrinth or did Calvin observe more grimly each man's mind *is* a labyrinth—she can't recall offhand and this summer she lacks the books she'd need to look it up.

After a short while the boys turn friendly, or almost. She'd counted on that.

She says, "Wouldn't anybody like to give me my first sharpshooting lesson?"—putting out her hand to the straw-haired boy who can't say but O.K.—"Yeh, O.K." He's embarrassed but also flattered. Eyes flashing up at her, warm and brown and flecked with sunlight, so vivid they look blind, like marbles. She sees his eyebrows and lashes are nearly white.

So. The first sharpshooting lesson of a life.

She does lay her bicycle down, stands as the boy instructs with her left foot boldly out, the rifle's stock snug but not tight against her right shoulder, head inclined, glasses sliding down her nose. Her left arm, supporting the rifle's barrel, is unsteady—is she trembling? Why is she trembling? The straw-haired boy tells her to squeeze the trigger, not to *pull* it or *jerk* it but to *squeeze*. He's a manly kid for his age, gallant. He'll grow to maturity quickly as in a photograph album where the snapshots flash forward with no heed for how the heart is rent. Don't pull don't jerk just squeeze says the boy take a slow breath and squeeze says the boy and, damn it, she jerks the trigger and the shot goes wild. You can't even hear a *ping!*—just silence.

One of the curly-haired twins snickers but the boy who is her friend takes the rifle from her and cocks it—a swift deft movement she doesn't quite catch—and hands it politely back, says, "Try again."

So she does. And another shot goes wild. And he says, "Nah—like this," and shows her how *he* does it and she watches keenly noting the sweaty rivulets on his chest and back, the deep-tanned heat of his flesh, those eyes that look lashless—just eye. He hands her the rifle and she takes it, imitating his stance, his confidence, she aims for a green bottle atop a mound of sun-glinting debris and though she's distracted for a moment by a monarch butterfly drifting through the scope she waits until her aim is reasonably steady and shuts her left eye and opens wide her right and does not jerk or pull the trigger takes her time takes a deep slow breath and as she inhales she squeezes the trigger and this time the shot flies out to shatter the bottle instantly, there's a gratifying *ping!*—the boys seem pleased, congratulatory. "Just a lucky accident," she says modestly, blinking, short of breath, and the boy says, "Nah, you got the knack—try a few more." He's generous and swaggering a little and of course she accepts his offer, standing with her left leg forward, her toes in the straw sandals digging in tight, such tension, such precision, her right eye up close to the tiny scope and her senses sharpened to the point very nearly of pain. She sees that, once you begin, you wouldn't ever want to stop.

Tick

She said, I can't live with you under these conditions, and her husband said, But these *are* the conditions. And moved out. And did not telephone her for several days. And when he did call she told him quickly, I'm happy here alone—I've gotten through the worst of it. Don't spoil my happiness again.

Since then the telephone rings at odd hours and she never answers. She will never answer—it's that simple. She does her work in the apartment spreading her books and papers out on the dining room table and she is working well, better than she has in years but it's all precarious, she knows it's precarious, not the temptation to kill herself—she understands this is an adolescent fantasy and would never act upon it—but the temptation to succumb to thoughts of despair, self-hatred. Easier, she thinks, to hate yourself than to respect yourself: it involves less imagination.

Tonight, contemplating these matters, she runs her fingers through her hair and comes upon a small bump on her head, the very crown of her head. A pimple, except it isn't a pimple. A mysterious hardness, shell-like. Could it be a tiny pebble embedded in her scalp? But how? She tries gently to dislodge it with her fingernails but it is stuck fast. What can it be?—she's fastidious about grooming, shampooing her hair every morning when she showers.

She tries to comb the thing out of her hair first with a plastic comb and then with a fine-toothed steel comb her husband left behind. It won't budge. Perhaps it is a tiny wound, a tiny scab, she thinks, and then she thinks, It's alive, it has its jaws in me. And she realizes it must be a tick.

Since her husband moved out and it is possible for her to go for days without seeing anyone she has made a conscientious effort to be better groomed than she has ever been in her life. Shaves her underarms before the harsh stubble appears, keeps her legs smooth and hairless. Always dresses no matter the black rain falling against the windows in the early morning and the faint odors of garbage and wet ashes pervading the apartment building. Puts on lipstick, sometimes even a touch of cologne on her wrist, behind her ear. Pride! she thinks, winking in the mirror. Self-reliance! There you go!

She's in the bathroom trying desperately to inspect the top of her head in the medicine cabinet mirror. Roughly parting her hair, stooping, her eyes rolling up in their sockets. But she can't see—it's impossible. She runs for a hand mirror and holds it at such an angle that she can see into the cabinet mirror where she parts her hair clumsily with the fingers of one hand and she gives a little scream and nearly drops the mirror: it *is* a tick, bloated and purplish-black, stuck fast in her scalp.

She instructs herself to be calm. Not to panic. Not to give in to nausea, gagging. It's only an insect after all, one of those tiny black spiderlike things, parasites that suck animal and human blood, it's said the woods and fields are filled with them because of the rain this spring, and the heat, or is it because of the dryness and the heat, they're remarkably quick, darting and leaping and flying, raining from the trees onto unknowing human heads which is how she must have picked this one up—walking through the park the other morning, forcing herself to look and to really *see* the beauty of the natural world which she'd lost these past several months or has it been these past several years, embarked upon the precarious enterprise of adult-hood, wifehood, loneliness.

She recalls that ticks secrete an anesthetic when they bite so you can't feel the bite. She recalls they're so hardy they can't be killed by ordinary methods, can't be squashed—the most practical method is to flush them down the toilet.

She is digging furiously at her scalp with her nails and the sink is flecked with blood, her blood, and a number of hairs. No reason to panic but she can't stop the frantic digging, she's bent low over the sink, panting, cursing, blood beating in her eyeballs and rivulets of sweat running down her back. She feels a sensation of nausea, a taste of something hot and acid at the back of her mouth but she manages to swallow it down. She thinks of the book she'd been planning to read this evening and the piano pieces by a contemporary composer whose work she admires she'd planned to study and work out though she hasn't a piano in the apartment yet (she intends to buy one, or rent one, soon, now that she'll have more time for it, and more energy) and these activities strike her suddenly as remote, preposterous.

Her husband once had a medical handbook, she goes to look for it in the bedroom in a pile of books he left behind but can't find it, she tries the bookshelves in the living room then the stack of books in the kitchen beside the refrigerator, mostly paperbacks and shame-lessly dusty, and when she's about to give up she discovers it, *The Family Medical Companion,* thank God her husband was so angry and hurt, so eager to get away from her, he'd left it behind. With trembling fingers she opens it to the section "Insects" that begins, "Insects are both friends and enemies of man. Some simply annoy by their bites and stings, but a few carry disease-bearing microbes."

The paragraph on ticks is disappointingly brief. She reads that she should not try to yank the tick out of her skin since ticks embed themselves so snugly, part of its body will very likely remain and there's the chance of infection. She has her choice of several proce-dures: she can hold a lighted match or cigarette against the tick's back until it wriggles free; she can coat it with Vaseline, gasoline, kerosene, or turpentine; she can pick the tick off gently with a tweezers.

She tries the tweezers. Tries repeatedly, a dozen times or more, at the bathroom sink, until the tweezers slips from her numbed fingers. She's crying. Her face is flushed as if with sunstroke, her eyes in the mirror are those of a deranged woman. To her horror she feels, or believes she feels, the tick stirring in her scalp—enlivened, enraged, burrowing more deeply into her flesh. She wonders if it has the power to pierce the bone, to embed itself in her very brain.

She jams her knuckles into her mouth to muffle her screaming.

She's close to hysteria so she leaves the bathroom and paces about the apartment, from one room to another, one room to another, in an effort to calm herself. Minutes pass: she has no idea how many. She beats her hands softly together, the fleshy parts of the palms, she tries to breathe deeply and rhythmically, after all this is such a minor problem, hardly a matter of life and death, if worse comes to worst she can take a taxi to a hospital to an emergency room but what if they laugh at her there?—what if they're furious with her there?—her with her face like death, trembling and panting as if she'd been physically assaulted, *a mere tick embedded in her scalp.* More plausibly, she might go next door and ask for help from her neighbor—but when she envisions knocking at the door, handing the astonished young woman the tweezers and begging her to extricate the thing in her head, she knows she can't do it. She isn't acquainted with the woman even casually—she's a shy cold girl very like herself. When they meet in the foyer or in the elevator each smiles faintly and pointedly looks away thinking *Don't talk to me. Please. Not right now.*

Perhaps she should kill herself after all—it would be the easiest solution to all her problems.

By this time she's walking fast, on the verge of breaking into a run, can't stop! can't sit down! her heart beating wildly and her breath audible. At the crown of her head there's a hot piercing throbbing pain. Her fingernails are edged with blood. She's rushing from room to room, pacing, turning in tight corners like a trapped animal, hardly seeing where she's careening, her eyes filled with tears of hurt, rage, frustration, shame—this is what it comes to, she's thinking, this is all it comes to, and she's leaning in a doorway trying to get her breath trying to stave off an attack of faintness when she hears the telephone ring and understands it has been ringing for some time.

She heads for it like a sleepwalker, propelled by a rough shove. She foresees a reconciliation, lovemaking both anguished and tender. She foresees starting a child. It's time.

Photographer's
Model

She was just a young girl, she says, nine, ten years old, when her uncle
started taking pictures of her, displaying them in the filling station
he managed or selling them to the local newspaper, then later to
magazines, so that she started seeing herself in print and that changed
her way of looking at herself forever. It wasn't that she was so pretty,
which she was, big eyes, curly hair, legs long and just right, something
nimble, monkeyish, about her, but she knew the primary fact, the
model's eye locked to the eye of the camera which is the eye of the
world. How she knew, how old she was when she knew, she can't say,
just something I was born with I guess like the color of my eyes.
Daddy was a deacon in the Sourland Methodist Church, had a small
dairy herd, a dozen Guernseys, but they were always poor, he was
always injuring himself outdoors, so they sent the two youngest
children (of seven) to live with his wife's brother in town. She hardly
missed the farm, she says, a few days and she was over missing it, she
never did give a damn for how her parents disapproved of her profession, nothing she did would've been right in their eyes, so let it go.
She and her Uncle Billy got along right away, really understood each
other. Big tall soft freckled good-natured man, managed a Sunoco
station but his love, he always said, was photography, spoke of himself as "free-lance" and everybody had to grant he really was good

but they supposed there was a trick to it, or just a special kind of camera, made in Japan.

She knew right away she wasn't like other girls her age, there had to be something special about her. Things Billy said. Things people said. The way she was in the photographs—herself but not only herself, somebody important, with secrets. Always a smile, something about the eyes, something knowing. And of course the legs. Her legs were to be her strong suit. A face you can experiment with, hair you can fix any number of different ways, but the legs have to be perfect and hers were. Fourteen years old, says Billy, and hers were. They started winning contests. He had her pose in jeans, playsuits, bathing suits, nothing crude or tacky, there were a few nudes but he decided not to send them out. One of the magazines paid $200. Another $500. Billy split it all with me which isn't what they usually do, photographers. Some of them are such bastards.

First time I pulled on black textured stockings, stood in three-inch heels looking at myself in the mirror, I must've been fifteen years old and I almost fainted at what I saw. Just stared and stared, looking at myself from the rear. Jesus I knew I had it then, I really knew. It sort of scared me.

Billy wouldn't speak to me for years, it hurt him that I made decisions on my own, moved away. Later he came round, now he's dead and it's a pity. Though maybe he sort of knows—I mean maybe he's aware. I think if there's a life after death he's aware of how things turned out for me.

No, hot lights don't bother, you get used to them unless you're working with another model which can be uncomfortable. Your powder gets gummy. Posing's the easiest thing in the world 'cause it's the most practical. You got a set time, more or less. You got a contract most of the time. That's not like other things in life where there's no purpose.

Sure I had some hard times, everybody does. A photographer's model or anybody, you got to expect some hard times, right? The fulfillment's in the work.

What I did hate, I guess, when I had to do it, was life classes. You know—posing for "artists," demeaning yourself in public. They sit you on a chair or something and nobody talks. Just staring at you, using you, like you were shit and weren't human. The men were actually the worst. Assholes that make you deliberately unattractive 'cause that's "artistic," right? Breasts sagging when they're not, legs shorter than they really are, face all smudged or crosshatched with pencil, thinking they're Picasso or somebody. But the photographer wants you to look good, he wants you to look real good, he wants to sell his pictures, he's naturally on your side.

Though some of them can be bastards. A contract doesn't guarantee everything.

My daddy used to say it's the work of the devil et cetera but nobody believes that kind of shit now. Actually I don't know what him and my mother think these days 'cause I broke off contact with them a long time ago. Also most of my sisters and brothers. They just don't understand, living where they do. If it isn't the country it's some little town, they say crude things about you or start acting friendly then you know: Watch out! Always needing money to get a new car, pay some hospital bill or something, they got fantastic hick ideas how much a photographer's model makes which is none of their business anyway.

Uncle Billy used to counsel me, Honey, just forget that bunch, who needs them?—they don't have your welfare at heart. 'Cause they know you're superior. 'Cause they know you're going way beyond them.

Like when I was fifteen and we won the first important contest and Billy said, Here we go, kid! Or even earlier, when the first pictures came out in the town paper and everybody complimented me, even the kids at school that hated me. And I knew that was what I wanted.

And I knew that was why I was born. That I could turn a page somewhere and see myself like it was by accident. That people were looking at me and people were talking about me. That they had to—'cause that's how it was.

Only thing I guess I really regret, Billy isn't alive right this minute. He'd be so proud. He's the only goddamn one. Those years when we weren't speaking, I didn't even send him a Christmas card or anything, all that would be forgotten now. Billy would just look at me smiling his big funny smile like we put over something on somebody, he'd say, Jesus, kid, you got it all now, don't you?

Accident

FOR   R. B.

A few days before Christmas years ago he was driving crosstown to the house his wife rented, the car windows rolled up tight, the radio on high, he was singing loudly and happily and with no mind for the brash yearning flatness of his voice since, alone, he wasn't being observed and had no need to feel self-conscious, or foolish. He and his wife had been separated for three tenuous months but these past several weeks they'd been tender and forgiving of each other: she loves him she says and he certainly loves her but (she says) marriage is so intimate there's no room to breathe is there? it's intimacy of this kind that frightens her though he guesses, or knows, that it's the precarious dialectics of intimacy with *him* that frightens her. (He's the one who loves her too much, wants too much from her, or from any woman: or this is the story he consoled himself with, those years—an excess of love, not a deficiency.) In any case as he drove in the lightly falling snow crosstown to the house in which his wife now lived with their four-year-old daughter he was singing as he'd recall afterward at the top of his lungs thinking of the evening ahead and its prospects—romantic, hopeful—as if (as if he knew nothing!) everything lay ahead, and nothing *past.* He liked it enormously that this long day—this week, month, year—was shifting inexorably to a hazy warm-wintry December dusk in a city he believed he knew yet which had the capacity still to surprise him, side streets unfamiliar to his eye and back alleys and vacant weedy lots and this twilit sepia look that through the windshield of his car (the '74 Chrysler) had a drunken feel to it though he wasn't drunk, hadn't had a drink yet that day. In the backseat a hefty bag of groceries and two bottles of good white Italian wine and his wife would smile surprised with pleasure, or with its necessary pretense. Tonight would be a celebration of sorts like certain nights lately when neither of them knew if he would stay with her, if he'd be invited to stay or want to stay, if invited, it depended upon an equilibrium of forces too subtle and too powerful to be named. He was thinking of these things when he began to notice that the car directly ahead of him was being driven erratically, he could see there was a couple in the front seat and it looked as if they were quarreling so he should keep his distance but he was impatient to get to where he was going since with that woman there was always the possibility of a misunderstanding . . . how quickly they occurred, those misunderstandings with his first wife, how bitter, and bewildering, and always, seemingly, irrevocable . . . and when he arrives the house is dark and locked against him and there isn't even one of her notes taped to the door *I love you but I don't want to live with you* or *I love you but I'm afraid of you* or *I love you isn't that enough can't we leave each other alone?*—and the car ahead of him stopped short at a railroad crossing, brake lights flashing red and he slammed on his own brakes immediately but his front wheels slid on the freezing pavement and he couldn't avoid hitting the rear bumper of the other car. It wasn't really a collision, a scratch or dent at the most, he wasn't going to lose his temper as he sometimes did, or had in the past, hot-blooded, people spoke of him though not without endearment if they were people he'd never seriously hurt but in any case this certainly wasn't his fault and he hadn't any time to waste so he tried to pass the car and the car jerked forward as if to block him so he paused thinking he didn't want trouble, swallowing hard against the dryness in his mouth thinking Jesus Christ not tonight. He tried then to pass the car on the right (though it was tricky driving over the railroad ties and in gravel risking a flat) but again the car lurched forward to block him and this time there's no mistaking it's deliberate. So he's sitting in the Chrysler the radio turned high playing a syncopated tinny Christmas carol and the other driver—a tall burly black man—is headed back to speak with him and he rolls the window down leaning out meaning to explain politely but without apology what happened—the sudden stop, the brakes, the slippery pavement, etc.—but without a word the black man simply punches him in the face. With a big balled fist like a rock.

Punches him so hard his head swivels with the impact of the blow and his neck is a stalk easily broken and there's no time for him to understand what has happened: though, afterward, he'll have a vague confused memory of a black man in his forties, coatless, hatless, unshaven, big horsey staring eyes and a flat thick nose and that look of derision, fury, utter contempt as he stooped and swung his fist with unerring accuracy into the white man's uplifted face . . . then turned, walked back to his car, drove away.

At first he wiped at the blood with both his gloved hands not knowing how much of it there was, and would be, not knowing what he did—desperate to keep the blood from staining his new topcoat and, since the coat was unbuttoned, his new mohair sweater. A trickle of blood or maybe a stream, fairly serious bleeding from his nose especially but it was just a nosebleed and wouldn't last long, then he discovered that one of his front teeth was slightly loose in its socket trying to soak the blood in clumps of Kleenex his heart pounding and sweat breaking out everywhere on his body thinking how had it happened?—he must have been thrown forward against the steering wheel. Slamming on his brakes as he had and his car stopped short and he'd struck the goddamned steering wheel but his nose didn't seem to be broken and his tooth wasn't actually knocked out and in the morning he'd call a dentist and see what could be done telling himself with a father's sober practicality—remembering now he *was* a father, loved his little girl very much though his love for her, his very sense of her, was somehow obscured by his passionate love for the woman who was her mother as if by that woman's actual physical presence obscuring, or protecting, the child—told himself it could be worse, much worse as he continued driving more cautiously now, over the railroad tracks and along the darkened potholed street toward a brightly lit street a few blocks ahead. He drove with one hand and with the other held a wad of tissue against his nose and mouth— wasn't yet feeling the pain he supposed he would feel when the shock wore off but the primary thing is, he told himself repeatedly, it could have been much worse.

When he got to his wife's he said as soon as she opened the door, quickly, guiltily, "I had an accident—hit my mouth on the steering wheel—it isn't serious—" as his wife cried, "Oh God you've been fighting again—" in a voice despairing and angry yet resigned, a voice he well knew. She stepped back from him, pointedly did not embrace him, their daughter was hiding behind her Oh Daddy Daddy *Daddy* and his heart was torn but after he cleaned himself up and they saw he wasn't really hurt and he had time to explain carefully what happened how he'd almost struck a car stalled on a railroad crossing, how he'd been thrown forward and his his mouth on the damned steering wheel though he'd been wearing his seat belt and you would think, wouldn't you, that might make a difference?—wearing a seat belt might make a difference?—things seemed to be all right. He was blinking back tears trying to control his voice which sounded like no voice he recognized but eventually it seemed his wife understood, he'd only had an accident, and a very minor accident, he hadn't been drinking and hadn't been in a fight and the night wasn't inexorably lost, or wasn't lost yet. After the first bottle of wine his wife touched his wounded mouth tenderly saying What a shame, an accident just before Christmas: and your new clothes. And he gripped her hand hard in gratitude whispering yes, what a shame, thinking of the shock he'd given her and the child when they trusted him, and thinking of his new clothes, blood-splattered and probably ruined, and the long night, or nights, ahead.

Mule

She was told to leave the house, just please leave me alone will you, Momma said. I want to hang myself and you're in the way.

Momma's a joker. Joker in the deck, you never know where it's going to turn up and what the hell it means.

(Actually Momma had some serious ambition along those lines. Signed up one winter at the community college for something called "The Art of Comic Performance" but dropped out midway 'cause it wasn't what she'd hoped for—mainly film clips of these old dead comics Charlie Chaplin, Buster Keaton, Marx Brothers, etc. Crap theory as Momma called it when what she wanted was lessons in joke-telling, information about how you get an agent, bookings in night clubs, *money.*)

Junie wasn't going to ask why Momma wanted to hang herself this time. There was some old greasy hemp rope on the cellar stairs one of Momma's ex-boyfriends had left a year ago, Why's *that* there Junie asked a thousand times and Momma'd just say Maybe I'll be using it some day, it's sort of like saving string. Junie'd make a sound like laughing, snorting—might as well since Momma liked for people to respond to her wisecracks even when she kept deadpan herself. Momma's personal theory about laughing is it sure beats crying. Right?

This new trouble—not that it was really new—had to do mainly with Buddy Bauer. Momma down at the sheriff's office trying to get what's called an injunction to keep the bastard from breaking down the door but the problem was (as Momma explained) once a man's been living under a certain roof and coming and going when he wants and, you know, sleeping in your bed, it's hard as hell to evict him and keep him evicted. That's when they turn mean.

Junie said to Momma, a little scream that turned into laughing, Why did you do this to us?—why *again?*

The first night Buddy came over he brought them Chinese takeout. Egg rolls and fried dumplings and sesame noodles and sweet-and-sour pork and Szechuan beef and God knows what all else, My God it's a feast Momma said. Always so surprised and happy when people, that is, men, were nice to her.

Later Momma would say: That's how they sucker you—a bucket of sesame fucking noodles!

Buddy was a truck driver, owned his own truck. Short-distance hauling: he wasn't going to pay union dues. Big-shouldered guy with a ham-sized face and a grin that split it up the middle. Salt of the earth Momma'd say, rubbing her bruises.

The thing about Buddy was, he liked to pinch—grown women, girls Junie's age, little kids who couldn't get away in time. That big thumb of his and fat forefinger and wide white grin—Junie had to be fast to elude him. It's just his way Momma insisted, maybe he misses his family. Junie thought, hearing this, *I* miss my family.

(In fact all she had was Momma—and all Momma had actually was her.)

Except here was Buddy Bauer—moved right in Momma's bedroom and his fishing gear, crotch-high rubber boots and other crap in the cellar. He's paying his own way Momma said. Helping out with the rent. Junie said, Sure Momma. Rolling her eyes and thinking, Die die die.

But Buddy *was* funny, sort of: one night sitting around the kitchen table drinking beer and eating cold pizza this long wild story about a mule corpse floating in some creek, floating and bobbing trapped under a bridge, and one of Buddy's cousins got him to dive in the water and Buddy slammed right through the corpse! and Junie laughed saying, God that's *gross,* but couldn't figure out when the stunt took place, how long ago, and where. She guessed the point of it was that Buddy hadn't been able to exactly see the mule corpse which was decayed and rotten and swarming with maggots and half eaten by fish 'cause it was floating under the surface of the water—but he told the story so poorly, he hadn't made that clear. It just sounded like some asshole diving into a dead mule then roaring with laughter over it. And Momma stared at Buddy like she'd never seen him before even her lips draining white and she got swaying to her feet and said in this weird voice, I think I'm going to be sick. They thought she was joking but when Momma ran for the bathroom gagging and vomiting in the hall they had to take her seriously.

Buddy pinched Junie on the soft skin inside her elbow and said, Your mother is a real sensitive lady. *She's* one of a kind.

That was last fall when they were all getting along. You never think a honeymoon's going to come to an end Momma said no matter how many you've tried.

(Poor dumb Momma rubbing her bruises. Makeup thick as pancake batter on her face.)

Now Buddy's been moved out for six weeks or more but his presence is much felt. Drunk telephone calls all hours of the night unless Momma leaves the phone off the hook—or he's waiting in his pickup truck at the end of the driveway, swilling beer in the dark. How many times can she call the sheriff's office?—it just wears you out Momma said. Oh Jesus Christ it wears you out like something getting thinner and thinner and *thinner.*

So now, 7:20 A.M., Momma in Junie's doorway in the same damn clothes she's had on for three days straight: shiny-seated black trousers, V-neck sweater showing the soft pale crepey crease between her

breasts, no shoes or stockings just dirty bare feet. Cries Momma, Rise
and shine! Up and at 'em! slapping her hands together and poor
Junie's woken not knowing where she is or what the hell's coming
down on her, one of those nightmares where she can't go forward or
back or even open her mouth to scream. Momma's talking a mile a
minute like she's high on something and giving off a heat too you can
feel so Junie cringes away pulling on her clothes saying O.K.
Momma, O.K. Momma. Momma's eyes look swollen, black with
pupil. Her laugh is high and piercing like a sliver in the heart.

All I want is some fucking privacy for once! Is that too much to ask!

Junie gets dressed shivering, teeth chattering, it's worse than any
nightmare 'cause she's awake and when you're awake you know it,
no escape. Momma's crazy tossing one-dollar and five-dollar bills at
her, sort of sailing them at her and across the bed. Go out and get
some decent breakfast, Momma says. You hear?

O.K. Momma.

Yours truly is signing off.

O.K. Momma.

Taking early retirement.

O.K. Momma.

Gimme a kiss before you go.

Junie lowers her head and allows the kiss. Tears leaking out the
sides of her eyes.

Go screw Momma, Junie says halfway out the door running down
the walk shoving her arm into the sleeve of her hand-me-down sheepskin jacket. Momma calls after her she should order the blueberry
special at the Pancake House but Junie doesn't look back. Mouth
tastes like the inside of a shoe and her head's not right. What time
is it? What day? Other times Momma tried to hurt herself—razor
blades, downers—she'd at least waited till Junie was in school.

(Your mother isn't serious they said. Junie wondered, Then what
is.)

She's trotting toward town—the neighbors' dogs start in barking.
Street lights still on and the sky is lightening to that pink-polar look

that sets your teeth on edge, so beautiful it hurts. The gravel road turns into a real street paved in asphalt with sidewalks, gutters, most of it cobbled with ice that's too dirty to glitter. There's a smell of something harsh and clean, though. A look of things being surprised by the new day.

Out here, thinks Junie, you stand a chance.

The Pancake House is too far so she settles for the diner by the bus station. Orange juice in a sticky little glass, griddle cakes soaked in maple syrup, two greasy fried eggs she shakes salt and pepper on before tasting. Coffee so hot and strong you almost can't taste it.

She's eating right there at the counter, head lowered, a strand of hair caught in the zipper of her jacket. So hungry it's a kind of happiness, just eating. Hungry for all you can get, Junie thinks. Wonders is it a line from a song.

That shit about the rope: O.K. *let her.*

This big guy with wooly hair, slow watchful smile, metal-rimmed glasses like some schoolmaster in a movie, he's sitting on the next stool over eyeing her not saying a word. No one Junie knows and no one who knows Momma otherwise he'd have said so by now, Momma's such hot shit with the boys. Finally he says like it took him this long to put together the words, Looks like somebody's having the works this morning—baring his big shiny teeth in a smile. Junie looks up squinting from her plate and smiles the sweetest smile of her own. Well—I'm learning, she says.

A Touch of the Flu

For years she tried to conceive a child, and failed; and failed at the marriage too—though "failed" is probably the wrong word, since, wanting a child so badly, and, as some observers (including her husband) said, so irrationally, she simply decided to give up on that man, and move on to another. And so she did; and conceived within months; and had her baby, a little girl; and lived with her alone, since, by that time, she'd come to understand that there was no room in her life for both the baby and the baby's father. Even had he wanted to marry her, which was not so clearly the case.

And she was happy with her little girl, if not, as she'd anticipated, ecstatic; except of course in bursts of feeling; wayward, unexpected, dazzling, and brief. These are the moments for which we live, she thought. She wondered if anyone had had that thought before her.

That summer she brought her daughter to Maine, to her parents' summer home, and there, each morning, pushed her in a stroller along the beach. She sang to her little girl, talked to her almost continuously, for there was no one in the world except the two of them, and, by way of the two of them, their delicious union, the world became new, newly created. She held her little girl in her arms, aloft, in triumph, her heart swelling with love, exaltation, greed. Sand, ocean, butterfly, cloud, sky, do you see? Wind, sun,—do you feel?

But one day she was overcome by a sensation of lightheadedness, and exhaustion, and returned to the house after only a few minutes on the beach, and handed the baby over to her mother, and went to bed; and did not get up for ten days; during which time she did not sleep, nor was she fully awake; simply lying in bed, in her old girlhood bed, her eyes closed, or, if open, staring at the ceiling, sightless and unjudging. Her mother brought her little girl to nurse, and she pushed her away, in revulsion, and could not explain; for it was herself she saw, in her mother's arms, as it had been, so suddenly, herself she'd seen, in her little girl, that morning on the beach; and she thought, I cannot bear it. Not again.

Still, the spell lifted, as such spells do. And she got up, and was herself again, or nearly; and nursed her baby again, with as much pleasure as before; or nearly. Her mother looked at her hard and said, "You've had a touch of the flu," and she smiled, and regarded her mother with calm wide intelligent eyes, and said, "Yes, I think that was it. A touch of the flu." And they never spoke of it again.

Holiday

The previous Christmas, shortly after they'd met, she and her lover had flown to Acapulco for twelve days, now she and her lover and her lover's twelve-year-old son were flying to Jamaica for two weeks, they had reservations in the best inn on the island, in fact her lover had stayed there once before, not with his family but at a conference. I can't leave my son this year, he told her, and I obviously can't leave you.

The son's name was Josh but it was a name, perhaps it was a sound, she couldn't bring herself to pronounce. He was tall for his age but otherwise underdeveloped, with a small head, skinny chest, arms and legs that looked too long for his body. She understood that he was a disappointment, a very slight disappointment, to her lover, because of his mediocre grades at school. He went to a first-rate prep school in Connecticut but he wasn't a boarder, the mother drove him back and forth each day, that was the reason most likely for his mediocre grades, but her lover didn't want, he said, to press the issue yet. The boy was only twelve, things wouldn't get crucial for another three, four years. He could wait. In the meantime neither parent discussed the other with Josh, they had learned to be diplomatic in their mutual hatred.

There was some initial awkwardness in getting the boy to meet her. He blamed her, her lover said, for the breakup, though in fact he'd

explained to the boy that it wasn't her fault, for how could it have
been her fault when Daddy had moved out of the house months
before he and she had met . . . ? So her lover drove her up to West
Hartford one Saturday in October to introduce her to the boy. He was
scheduled for a tennis lesson at 10:00 A.M. and when they arrived at
the tennis club at 10:20 the boy must have sighted them approaching
the court because he ran off, hid away in the clubhouse, refused to
come out to meet her. Her lover was inside with him nearly an hour.
During this time she waited on the grass, watched the other tennis
players, walked around, then went back to the car to sit with the door
open and the radio on. She told herself it was too beautiful a day, one
of those blue October days, to be upset.

When her lover came out the boy wasn't with him. This was the
wrong day for it, her lover said. He apologized for his error in
judgment. He'd spent a long time in there, he said, his face flushed,
apologizing to his son.

Eventually they met. She remembered afterward shaking hands with
the boy, his limp cold ungiving fingers, she remembered smiling and
asking him bright harmless questions about school, tennis, but she
couldn't remember his answers. When he stayed at her lover's apartment in the city she had to move her things into a small guest room
with a studio couch and boxes of unpacked books stacked against the
walls. In the boy's room there was a television set, he brought along his
own phonograph, played records, loud, for hours. What is the point of
spending a weekend with us, her lover asked, if he hides away like this?
The boy also placed calls to his mother back in Connecticut. As if, her
lover said, he wouldn't know, when the phone bill came due.

On the evening before they were scheduled to fly to Jamaica the
boy came into the kitchen where she was preparing dinner. He wore
jeans that seemed to emphasize the thinness of his legs, a sports shirt
that fitted him poorly about the shoulders, jogging shoes with the

laces untied. His hair was combed, he was smiling nervously. She asked him if he had packed all his things, if he was ready for tomorrow, she addressed him as Josh. He was holding a bottle of 7-Up which he offered to her, Want some? and she said without thinking, All right, thanks, but when she took the bottle from him, lifted it to her mouth, she could smell what was inside and handed it back to him. That isn't funny, she said, that isn't funny at all, she said, but he was out of the kitchen before she started to cry.

She said nothing about the incident to her lover, it would have been an error in judgment, nothing to be gained, and on the eve of their holiday. He felt, sometimes, he told her, as if his mind were fracturing, parts of his personality breaking off, flying in all directions. He loved her, for instance, yes he adored her, she understood that, but there were other kinds of love, many other kinds of obligation, God knows. And she saw the helplessness in his face. And she saw the faint raw red rim of anger, in his eyes. So she said nothing about the incident with the 7-Up bottle, it would be her secret, hers and Josh's, she thought, a bond between them.

Early on the morning of their flight to Jamaica, before dawn, five-thirty, the sky outside her window pitch-black, and she lies beneath the comforter, alone, warm, snug, her lover is asleep in his room, Josh is presumably asleep in his, no one has to be out of bed until seven o'clock: she will be safe for hours. She remembers school mornings when she woke with a sore throat, a runny nose, her mother refused to allow her to go to school, she'd sit up in bed with extra pillows behind her, the big fuzzy quilt from her mother's bed, she would read, she would nap, she would draw, her mother might come sit on the edge of the bed and they'd play cards or Parcheesi, the joy grew and grew through an entire morning, never in her adult life has she been so happy. That's all I ever wanted, she thinks. That was enough.

Eleuthéria

Locally it was known as the villa, enviously, half-sneeringly, the large white Greek Revival house built above the lake at its widest point where the narrow body of water, meager elsewhere, had the look of a self-contained sea. Water forever in motion, churned to white in rough weather but a blue mirroring the sky most of the time, quiet, ordered, murmurous—beauty to lacerate the soul. And the rich man's house above. And the tiered garden with its Oriental pretensions. And the dock, the sailboat larger than any he'd seen before, the flapping sailcloth dazzling white in the sun, the smooth gleaming keel, the mysterious word *Eleuthéria* in black script he shaped with his lips too shy to say aloud even to himself. Sun explodes in handfuls off the slow-rocking water and he's dizzy, drunk, elated knowing that in another minute someone will begin shouting for him to get away, go back where he came from, a man in white trousers and a white shirt descending the hill clapping his hands at him as if to scare away a stray dog. . . .

And he runs, he's quick. He's used to it. He's quick.

Seventy years later he's being told that he must not insist upon cremation and his ashes scattered because those who love his work will want a specific place, a shrine . . . like James Joyce's grave in Zurich, like Proust's, Keats's. . . . You can't mean to deprive them, he's told.

Certainly not, he says, laughing. Oh certainly not!

It is a birthday celebration, a public event, he's being honored for a "lifetime of achievement" he knows he hadn't any choice but to do but he'll accept the honor nonetheless, he's kindly, tactful, patient, almost worthy of the love his younger contemporaries, who didn't know him in his youth, bear for him. So he sits smiling and solemn enduring the toasts, the praise, the effusive claims, guessing he has crossed over safely into mythology of a kind, he'll endure for a while after his death. He thinks of a boy being chased: the tall sailboat looming above him in the sunshine: *Eleuthéria* in flowing black script against the spotless white . . . and though it has been years, decades, since he has known what the word means it is still mysterious to him, and gravely beautiful, like the names of the dead.

And sweet, he thinks, though his enemies are long vanished. He couldn't hope to say, how sweet.

The Abduction

She was seventeen years old and mature for her age and she'd known
of course what the word meant but would not have applied it to what
happened to her one afternoon when, not exactly hitchhiking along
the highway by the shopping mall, just walking there, alone, her
shoulders hunched against the wind, she was asked by this man
driving a low-slung rust-speckled Cadillac would she like a ride, so
she said sure, and got in the car, and it wasn't actually right away
that she understood something was wrong though that's what she
would say afterward and perhaps even, with the passage of days,
weeks, months, come eventually to believe, but when he started in
talking kind of strange and making little jokes hardly talking *to* her
or asking questions of the kind she and her girlfriends usually were
asked by guys like this, meaning men that were older, clearly past
thirty and in this case (she'd looked at him climbing in, got a good
clear look at him and wasn't put off by what she saw, just a guy with
a pocked or pitted skin the kind you naturally feel sorry for, and hair
going thin on top this gunmetal-gray like her father's wetted down
and combed carefully so the balding spots didn't show, or didn't show
much, and some sort of twitchy little moustache she'd have laughed
at with her girlfriends but he was wearing what looked like a nice
topcoat and had a tie on, and a white shirt which men hardly wear

anymore not even the men teachers at the high school, and there was something about, what was it, his hands, his fingers, the nails that were specially clean, clipped short and neat and filed)—when he kept on talking in this queer voice like he was making an effort not to talk too fast or get too excited and wasn't paying all that much attention where he was driving, which lane exactly was he in, and which speed he wanted—fast, or slow—and the things he was saying didn't make all that much sense if you tried actually to listen to them (he seemed to be angry about the U.S. Government because he'd been cheated, he said, of something, or somebody had betrayed him, and there was a lot too about Christmas and this time of year and ghosts out of the ancestral past pushing forth he said in the genes of the living, the genes and chromosomes—which she picked up on because they'd been studying that kind of thing in biology) then she knew she'd made the worst mistake of her life climbing into a car with a crazy man and was he going to rape her? was he going to murder her? Her blood did truly run cold, icy-cold, all that stuff is true when you're scared to death, her fingers and her toes cold like a corpse's and her heart, dear God her heart was beating so hard and fast it seemed like it was going to push out of her chest rocking her entire body while she sat there trying to smile listening to this madman talking and talking and talking as he'd do for the next hour and twenty minutes though she tried to tell him she wanted to get out of the car, she had to get home where they were waiting for her and he was taking her out of her way please she begged please mister would he stop and let her out starting to cry a little so he reached over and touched her for the first time which almost freaked her out but he was saying how he wouldn't hurt her for the world, he was a pacifist and would never hurt another living sentient being unless he was forced but she would have to sit still she couldn't make him nervous while he was driving or they might have a fatal accident so she sat as quiet as possible staring straight ahead but not really seeing anything for a while so it came as a kind of surprise when she realized they weren't on Route 1 anymore but on I-95 going over into Pennsylvania and he was talking

like before but talking faster with this excitement you could almost
feel in the air around him like radiant heat, the moral crimes of the
U.S. Government and certain curses out of the ancestral past, and he
was weaving from one lane to another so she thought they'd have an
accident and both be killed, then what was worse he suddenly got
sleepy yawning and shaking his head and slapping at his cheeks to
keep awake and he told her it was fatigue like battle fatigue, trench-
warfare fatigue had she ever heard of that? and she said no and he
said Well it's a phenomenon of mental life you're in the trenches in
the foremost line of fire and you fall asleep so maybe she should sing
to him to keep him awake to keep from having an accident and she
asked why didn't he put on the radio and he said he didn't have a
radio, so she tried to sing, her voice faint and sickish and her throat
scratchy so the words died out after a few minutes but he didn't seem
to notice, maybe hadn't been listening, still yawning and slapping at
his cheeks smelling of sweat giving off this weird heat and they were
going eighty miles an hour so fast the car rattled over the bridge over
the Delaware into Pennsylvania then toward Philadelphia and she was
wondering could she signal somehow for help, could anyone guess the
situation she was in or would they just naturally think she was a girl in
a car with her father, even if she was crying, looking so scared, but if
anybody glanced at her they didn't actually see her, it was clear they
didn't give a damn about her, barreling along in this guy's old Caddie
past Philadelphia and past Wilmington, Delaware, and into Maryland halfway to Baltimore when the gas gauge showed empty and the
little red light went on in warning and he said he would have to stop
for gas and would she promise him to stay still in the car and not
cause him to hurt her and she said yes she promised but he didn't exit
at the next exit as she'd expected, kept driving despite the red light
blinking on and off and on again until finally he had to stop, pulled
into one of the service stations and up to the gas pumps and she said
she had to use the restroom (which was true enough) and he said
would she promise him she'd come back and she said yes she'd only
be gone a minute or two and she was smiling to show him she was

telling the truth seeing how sweaty he was, the poor guy, hair gummy on his forehead and some of it coming loose so you could see the bald places, him saying she'd been so kind and patient and he could see in her eyes her special quality, hers was to be a special destiny he said so it was imperative *she return to him* and she said yes she would her fingers closing around the door handle and by this time the gas station attendant was rapping at his window and it was like a moment in a dream when something terrible and wonderful is happening, and so easily—she opened the door and climbed out and started to run sobbing and screaming for help and that was the way it ended, the abduction as it was called by police and in the newspapers and on the 6:00 P.M. Trenton news that very night and the next night too when she was a guest on the show interviewed live telling her story breathless and pretty remembering to look directly at the camera as they'd instructed her, the camera with the red light is the one that's on, were you frightened, did you think he would kill you, what sorts of things did he say to you, what sorts of things were going through your mind? and she answered as truthfully as possible as, in the days, weeks, months, and eventually years to come she would tell of that event in her life that was like nothing before it and nothing to follow when she'd known she was marked for a special destiny and a special happiness—about which, out of very gratitude, she dared not speak.

In Traction

C. was required to fly home from the American Academy in Rome to spend some time with her cousin A., who was said to be going through a difficult period. C. hadn't seen A. in years—she hadn't been home in years—and resented the fact that her cousin's "difficult period" was presumed to be more dangerous than her own.

As girls they were frequently mistaken for sisters, even for twins, but now, C. saw, shocked, that all that had changed. A. was thin, even gaunt, but walked heavily, with a slight limp; a queer ironic anger danced behind her eyes; her skin was tinged with yellow, and rather coarse, like aging paper. The story was that she had tried to kill herself—walking, drunk, across a bridge busy with traffic, late on a Saturday night, jumping, or falling, onto a concrete abutment fifteen feet below, injuring herself so badly (broken ribs, dislocated hip, sprained ankle, lacerations) she had to be hospitalized for several weeks. At first she insisted she remembered nothing of the incident, then she denied that she'd jumped: she must have been forced off the bridge by a car, she said. "Hell, I want to live," she said belligerently, "—same as everybody. Same as you." She grinned at C. as if challenging her to disbelieve, or believe. For C.'s arrival she had smeared bright red lipstick across her mouth and uncorked a bottle of champagne she lied about having found in the cellar, in the old cistern.

Most days, A. felt too depressed to move from the sofa. C. kept her
company though they rarely talked. The family believed that A. had
tried to kill herself—that she was drinking herself to death, in fact—
because of a man, some man, one or another of the various shadow-
men she'd been seeing recently—but C. soon realized that there
wasn't any man, no one of significance. A. had been married for five
or six years, in her twenties, and during that time she and C. had
forgotten each other, which seemed to C. both sad and logical. One
of life's minor satisfactions is forgetting. "Sure I want to live, same
as you," A. said several times, yawning, slitting her eyes at C. "Don't
you feel superior to *me,* sweetie." Perhaps she was joking, perhaps
it was a kind of flirtation. Like joy, C. thought, despair is infectious.

She was so immaculate a young woman, her own despairing moods
were now indistinguishable from her happy moods.

As a child of nine C. had broken her right leg in a sledding
accident—on a steep pasture hill a quarter-mile from A.'s house, in
fact—and for several terrible weeks she had been in traction in St.
Joachim Hospital, strung up on an aluminum frame of some sort, a
heavy white plaster cast running from her ankle to her groin. The leg
had been broken badly, a socket in the hip injured. Sometimes she
was in an agony of pain, sometimes in an agony of itching. It wasn't
just her leg that was in traction but her back, her neck, her entire
body, her head—pulled taut, tight, held suspended like a breath she
couldn't exhale. It was an amazing punishment C. forgot for years,
then began to remember, for no reason, in her early thirties, when she
frequently felt *in traction,* again for no clear reason. There was the
long, long breath you held and were going to exhale but couldn't:
even your fingers stretched, even the hairs on your head, your littlest
toes, peeping out bare at the end of the great white cast. A. had come
to visit her in the hospital several times, urged by her mother, no
doubt, and bringing a present each time—the only one C. could recall
was a bridal doll in gossamer white with a gorgeous bouffant hairdo,
jet-black as Elizabeth Taylor's or Mrs. Elvis Presley's, and simpering
little rosebud lips. The doll must have been chosen by A.'s mother

since A. was as reluctant to give it to C. as C. was in accepting it: of course C. detested dolls, she wanted only books or drawing and watercolor supplies. In the hospital room the cousins faced each other with nothing much to say. C. wished hotly that A. were in her place so that *she* could walk out and never come back.

Now her wish had come true but she took no pleasure in it, she was too grown, too adult.

It was said of A. by the relatives that she didn't keep herself clean, didn't bathe, wash her hair, see to her fingernails. That she drank on the sly even when company was in the house. That she kept the blinds drawn even in the daytime, was careless about washing dishes, making her bed, money. All these things were true, C. soon discovered, but what of it? When A. felt especially low C. washed her hair for her, combed it carefully (making no mention of the fact that hairs came out in considerable quantities in the comb); manicured her brittle fingernails (as she would never have troubled to manicure her own); even did the laundry (to the point of hanging out, on A.'s mother's old gray clothesline, the wash-and-wear shirtwaists and blouses of A.'s that looked best if allowed to drip dry). Once, in the second week of C.'s visit, A. insisted that C. join her in a glass of red wine, or two, and C. said why not, and the cousins sat in A.'s twilit bedroom, talking softly and idly, not talking, for some time. A. lay across the bed, her eyes closed, the back of one hand resting lightly on her forehead. Her breath was deep and steady. Her lips were pursed hard, raising little creases in her chin. C. was stroking her hair, then her shoulders, through her thin cotton bathrobe; she was disturbed by the prominence of A.'s collarbone, the two taut delicate bones at the base of her throat. A.'s eyelids fluttered but did not open. She said, "It was never the dangerous times that worried me. I could handle them. Emergencies. Getting sick. Some man making threats, or wanting to get married. It was daily life—the routine. *This* routine. I never learned."

"Why are you speaking in the past tense?" C. asked.

Her cousin didn't answer, perhaps hadn't heard. Outside on the highway a diesel hauled itself up a hill; the sound was remote yet jarring, as if it were coming from the next room. C. brushed A.'s hair off her forehead and let her hand rest there, lightly, for a few seconds. The skin was warm but surprisingly dry. A.'s breathing was as calm and measured as her own. She understood that A. was perfectly sane, rational, well, that she might or might not drink herself to death, she might or might not kill herself, accidentally or otherwise, it was not for C. to judge. Still, she would stay with her for as long as seemed required. Her own life, held in suspension, could wait; was waiting. She wondered how long A. might need her, how long this summer's visit would turn out to be—there was no reason, after all, for it ever to end.

Romance

He noticed her in the drugstore looking after him, then when he went out to his car she was standing there, waiting. Eighteen years old maybe. Straw-colored hair straggling down her back, round face, fattish cheeks, nervous little smile. Asked him which way he was driving along Huron Avenue and when he told her she asked for a ride, she was late getting home, she said, lived down past the traffic circle. She stood with her legs slightly apart, backs of her hands on her hips, posed-looking, chin uplifted, but her voice was breathy as if frightened. The request so took him by surprise, he couldn't have said no.

It was nearly dark, past eight o'clock, late July, warm, all day a heavy overcast sky, air difficult to breathe. The pills he took to lower his blood pressure slowed his heartbeat and made breathing more difficult. But it was nothing, he rarely thought of it now. In the light from the drugstore window the girl looked drained of color like an undersea creature, smiling at him. Did she know him? Should he have known her? Her lips were full and fleshy, very red, lifting from childish teeth. She was too old to be a friend or classmate of his daughter's, he knew better than to ask.

I'm late getting home, she said. Knew which car was his, went to get in, swung her hair off her shoulder, sat rather heavily. Big thighs

straining against pink cotton slacks, loose sleeveless muslin shirt, a
grayish white, so thin that her shadowy breasts were visible, almost
visible, inside. She was carrying a cheap straw bag, stuffed full of
things, she started rummaging through it right away, talking to herself, half scolding as if she'd lost something.

Scared as hell, she said, shivering, —getting home late.

They were driving along Huron, he was intensely aware of her,
rummaging through the bag, giving off a stale powdery heat. She kept
shifting her legs as if she couldn't get comfortable. Nails painted red,
shiny, slightly chipped, uneven. Grimy toes, pudgy little toes, in old
water-stained sandals. Squirming about like that she reminded him
of his children when they were younger but of course he couldn't tell
her to sit still. She said, Mister, it's awful kind of you, it's real sweet
of you, givin' me a ride home like this. It isn't just anybody that would
do it.

He would have liked to ask why she'd been hanging around the
drugstore, why she was late getting home, why scared, but instead he
said something about the weather, the humidity, it was a topic everyone talked of these days. She said at once, vehemently, Yeh it gets
me down, you got to have air conditioning or you can't hack it.

A moment later she said as if she'd just thought of it, I got me a
little unit, fits right in the window, you know?—so I can sleep at
night. Guy I know, got it for me from a discount place.

That's nice, he said.

Yeh it is nice, she said. People can be nice. Sometimes.

You got a cigarette? she said.

He told her no, he didn't smoke.

She seemed suddenly interested. Looked at him. You give it up, or
didn't you ever smoke? she asked.

Gave it up, he said.

Oh yeh? How long did you smoke? she asked suspiciously.

Seventeen years.

Jesus, seventeen *years.*

She spoke huskily, impressed. Then a moment later, in a half-teasing drawl: So how'd you quit the habit, mister, it's hard to do isn't it? Your wife make you stop or something?

He shrugged his shoulders. The conversation was making him distinctly uneasy.

She said with a self-satisfied little giggle, *Me* I got every bad habit there is, you can count 'em one two three four five. It's willpower you need to get off them, she said, like they say on the radio. That radio evangelist, you know? What's-his-name—WMWR—you ever listen to him? No? He's sort of interesting. She paused, then said: He's full of shit actually.

She began to hum under her breath. Wriggled in her seat, brought one knee up cozily beside her, lay her head back against the window. He knew she was looking at him, gazing, staring, in a way meant to provoke or to arouse. He kept on with his driving, looking ahead. But his heart was beating quite rapidly.

She said, I'm reading your thoughts, mister.

Yes? You are?

I am, she said, giggling. But I better not say.

She gave him directions at the traffic circle, her place was a block or so away. On a corner, upstairs over an upholsterer's shop. She said, You been awful sweet to go to this trouble, you want to come upstairs or something? Have a drink, or something?

He was saying no, thank you no, quickly, and she said, There's some cold beer in the refrigerator, and he said, suddenly sweating inside his clothes, It's late, I can't, thank you but I can't.

Now everything happened rather quickly.

They were parked in front of the upholsterer's shop, which was closed. The street was empty of traffic, a cloud of gnats and small moths swarmed dizzily about a street light close by. Hey why not come up for a while, mister, sure, have a drink, relax, she said huskily. Turn on the air conditioner: wow! She had begun to stroke his arm with canny wiry fingers. Digging in just slightly, teasing, with the nails.

He was aroused at once, he couldn't help himself. He said, half

laughing, shocked, Look really I *can't,* and she said, My name's
Rhonda and I think you *can,* stroking his arm, his thigh, kneading
the flesh. Her manner was playful yet urgent. They might have been
old, old friends. Look I *can't,* he said, his face flushed. The wild urge
to laugh nearly overcame him. This *is* where you live, isn't it?—you'd
better get out.

She said, pouting, stroking his thigh, You're going to let me go up
there alone?—hey I'm afraid of being alone right now.

It was all happening so swiftly, and so easily: not like a dream but
supremely, defiantly real. An ease and a naturalness entirely out of
place in his life. But he heard himself saying, half stammering, I'm
sorry. If this is where you live you'd better get out.

She must have known that he had no intention of coming with her
but she continued with her teasing, pouting, cajoling, baby talk, now
sly and lascivious, easing her hand between his legs, rubbing his groin
in small circular massaging movements. The situation was intoler-
able, ludicrous, comical, yet he thought it odd that he wasn't really
that shocked or surprised.

He shoved her away, slapped at her hand the way one slaps a
child's hand.

She was breathing quickly, heavily. Mouth a dark dramatic O, eyes
narrowed in a pretense of emotion. They were both very warm. Now
whining, hunching against him, she said that she was afraid to be
alone tonight, maybe they could go down the street, there was a place,
Smiley's, did he know Smiley's? no? well they could have a drink or
two there, get to know each other. It's no big deal, she said.

Please get out, he said.

Hey it's no big deal! she said. Relax.

He was trembling, aroused, a violent pulse beat in his groin.

But he heard himself speak calmly: Look, if you're frightened
about something, if someone is bothering you, I could take you to the
police.

She said, snorting, Oh hey no, no I can't.

He said, But is someone bothering you? A man?

She said, plump cheeks gleaming, a strand of hair in her mouth, Maybe yes and maybe no, mister, but the point is I don't want no asshole police messing me up.

He said, But is someone bothering you? Is someone waiting upstairs in your apartment?

She said at once, Oh no, mister, hell no, nobody's there, is that what you been thinking? No, Jesus, she said, we'd have the place to ourselves, that I guarantee. Okay?

He shoved her away again, more forcibly. He said, If you don't want to contact the police then I'll have to ask you to get out. Just get out.

She said savagely, Fuck you, mister.

Just get out.

She opened the door angrily. Slid out, hunched, her mouth sour, hair falling in her face. *Just get out!* she said in a mocking falsetto voice.

He thought of the girl obsessively for days, weeks.

Why, he didn't know. She'd only wanted money from him, most likely, she might even have intended blackmail, might have had a boyfriend, a pimp, waiting upstairs. She was crude, hardly attractive except for her youth. And that brashness. The smell of her. The head-on plunging, touching him as she had.

He had surprised himself too with his own response. It had all seemed so natural, so easy, he hadn't been shocked though of course he had been revulsed.

He drove by her apartment a half-dozen times that summer. Even by day the upholsterer's shop looked closed. An old wingback chair in the window, a bolt of faded fabric slung across the arms and seat. The building was two-storied, narrow, with shabby asphalt siding, an outside stairway, television antennas above. The blinds of the windows directly above the upholsterer's shop were always drawn. In one window there was a small cheap air-conditioning unit.

The street was busy enough by day—traffic, children playing noisily on the sidewalk—but no one came or went at the girl's place.

She'd been a prostitute, he might have seen that immediately and saved himself some embarrassment. Very likely too she'd been taking drugs. Slightly high, giddy. A skin that looked as if it were very warm. Damp close-set eyes . . . But what if she had simply been lonely, he wondered. They might have gone somewhere for a drink or two, no harm really, she wouldn't have known his name or how to contact him.

Once, at the end of August, driving past the upholsterer's shop, he happened to see a man leaning out of one of the upstairs windows. Sleepy-looking, unshaven, youngish, long straggly hair, T-shirt with the arms ripped off, scratching at his chest. But though he saw the man the man didn't seem to see him.

Only Son

But he has cousins, so many cousins. And then there are strange children in the park where sometimes his mother takes him if she's feeling strong, sometimes the maid in her white nylon dress—the fabric stretched tight over her fat breasts and hips, mysteriously shadowed by the dark flesh inside. Her accent is soft and husky and shy-sounding, Conchita is different, he is told, from the other maids who are just local niggahs: she's from Barbados. He stared down the smooth dark length of her arm to where she pointed at some little white girls wading in the pool, shrieking and splashing, barefoot, their panties showing. Ain't they somethin' now, ain't they the prettiest things! Conchita laughed. Afterward he tried to say how she said *ain't* but it was something like *amn't* and he couldn't get his tongue right. One day she showed him in secret a snapshot of her own little girl, skin black and looking as if it had been polished hard, just slightly pop-eyed staring back at him, her hair arranged in dozens of cornrows so tight they must hurt; or maybe, he thought, it was a little black doll, even the eyeballs polished. Conchita whispered, How'd you like to marry this sweet baby?—you an' her?—*ain't* she the darlinest thing—but he pretended not to hear.

His girl cousins were all older than he was. They petted him and fussed over him, took him away upstairs in his uncle's house and combed his hair funny ways, giggling in the mirror, they tried little vests on him, scarves, necklaces, at the big family picnic in August they pushed him on the swing, took him up on the slide, wandered away and forgot him but he was too proud to cry. His uncle was famous, he was told, throughout the world. Uncle had a special call from the Lord and the Lord had blessed him. At the big family picnic Uncle always stood to lead them in prayer, giving thanks to the Lord and to His Only Begotten Son for the food they were to eat and for a myriad of other blessings. Then the girl cousins stopped poking one another and giggling behind their hands, then they clasped their hands, bowed their heads like everybody else. He watched them, though, in secret. The parts in their hair. The little dewy patches on their bare arms.

At school he learned to watch the girls sidelong. They had so many different kinds of skin though they were all white like himself, their hair was so many different colors, fixed so many different ways. The boys' hair was all cut more or less alike: his was trimmed short. Later he knew to look at the sleeves of their blouses or dresses if the sleeves were short. If the armholes were big enough to peek through. That was how you could see inside their clothes without anybody knowing: the armhole. And sometimes at recess if they played rough he could see their thighs fast and blurred, looking smooth, the way his own were smooth. In his bed the girls ran and kicked and held hands playing whip the whip and the insides of his eyelids blazed with nasty heat.

In school the teacher went up and down the rows, asking, What would you like to grow up to be?—and he surprised them all by saying, A matador. And then the teacher had to explain what a matador was. And she said, But is that really what you want to be? and he felt sick because he'd been caught in a lie and now everyone would know, and he said in a whisper, I want to be a minister and serve the Lord.

In his room, though, he played at being a matador, he'd saved pictures from a magazine, spread out on the bed. The bull streaming blood, the tall lean young man with a red cloth like a flag in one hand, the deadly thin sword in the other . . . His mother found the pictures hidden in a drawer and took them away without a word.

He wasn't a child now, he knew certain facts, he was scornful, disgusted. Leafing hurriedly through magazines. Staring at the pictures. And there were girls and young women on the street. And in the park. And at the beach where his parents didn't like him to go by himself. At Bible Camp: the nonsense of the girls' cabins. Boys from his cabin sneaking out after dark to peek through their windows. He was scornful, disgusted, he held himself aloof, twice he had to ask to be assigned to another cabin, but he didn't tell Pastor Dill the reason why.

The last Sunday at Bible Camp, his uncle and his cousin Marilee were special guests. Marilee was nineteen years old now and she'd been on national TV singing gospels. Baby fat quivering in her cheeks, eyes uplifted to Jesus. He knew she wore glasses but never in public, she was too vain. His uncle preached, and Marilee sang "What a Friend I Have in Jesus" with her hands clasped hard together and tears starting in her eyes. Such a pretty girl, everyone whispered. Peaches and cream. Such a lovely girl. He listened to her and his stomach and groin tightened. He was staring at her where she stood next to the pulpit, dressed in white like a wedding dress, white satin ribbons, white gardenia in her hair, but everyone in the hall was staring. He didn't clap in rhythm with the others, though, when Marilee got them started. He didn't hear the words to the hymn because he already knew them. He just wanted to rip her apart with his teeth.

Bad Habits

Eighteen months into the marriage and he has begun sleeping until mid-morning, until noon, these windswept November mornings overlooking the Atlantic when life has got to strike you hard in the gut making you blink, and stare, My God here we all are: *existing!*—or you won't make it through the next hour. And she can't rouse him. And he doesn't want to be roused. Honey it's late, honey I have to leave for work, honey are you all right? Are you sick?—telling herself carefully that it *is* only sleep isn't it, heavy and protracted and smelling of death but still within the parameters of *sleep* some distance from *daze, stupor, coma.* No drugs and no alcohol. No husbandly exhaustion from overwork, overexertion. Once it was four or five hours he required somewhere in the dreamy center of her own unvarying seven hours, working at his desk late into the night (translations, poems) or curled happily at his end of the old leather sofa reading, annotating, scribbling inspired for hours with a child's complete absorption in whatever these matters are, these mysterious inaccessible counterworlds. A boy's fierce face, round wire-rimmed glasses with thumb-smudged lenses (she could see, sometimes, the thumbprint floating in his wide myopic gaze), you'd think twenty years old and in fact he is thirty-one and brilliant and she loves him except for these bad habits emerging one by one: for instance digging his nails into his scalp . . . poking his little finger into his ear and tugging, twisting . . . picking his nose compulsively . . . pinching his face and throat as if, unconsciously, or is it consciously, his fingers hope to stretch, ravage, scar. And sleeping. And sleeping all the time or so it seems and when he's awake his face is sleep-groggy, his eyes hooded with the memory or the anticipation of sleep, that solitude into which she cannot follow him, though the old sweet-startled smile can still be summoned if she breathes against the nape of his neck in passing or leans over his chair her arms draped around his neck or positions herself frankly in front of him, hugging him, knuckles locked together tight behind him, Honey is something wrong? What's wrong? I think you'd better tell me what's wrong? and he smiles or tries to, says softly, Nothing is wrong. Though once, relenting, guilt-ily: I don't know.

There he glides past in his stained chino trousers, the T-shirt and the black wool sweater unraveling at the cuffs, sometimes, even when the season turns, in this drafty "weatherized" beach house, barefoot: and there's no shadow to him! She thinks, The two of us *dead,* this is a *dead* place we came to, of our own volition. At the back of her head she sees the car making its bouncy way along the sandy rutted lane, sees the summery young couple carrying suitcases, boxes, cartons, clothes on hangers, the sun winking on the waves and the beach broad and reasonably clean and a smell of something brackish, wide-awake, exciting to the air, now he's yawning behind his hand or staring out the window at the sky that, changing, never changes, quantities shift, that's all—he says, simply: Quantities shift—and of course they never, or almost never, make love any longer. And when they do it hurts.

He sleeps afternoons too, or so she suspects.

From the community college forty-five minutes away where she teaches she telephones their number and there's no answer, just the ringing ringing ringing as if in an empty house, and she dials quickly a second time in case she had dialed incorrectly the first time, Damn you, oh please answer, I hate you, I *love* you, please answer, and then

an hour later (she forces herself to wait a full hour) she tries again
and again there is no answer, and she's beginning to be frightened,
no she isn't really frightened, she knows he is all right, he is simply
in one of his moods, private, stubborn, not even hostile to her, simply
apart from her and exclusive of her, or perhaps (she tells herself) he
is at his desk working, concentrating, doesn't want to be disturbed,
covering folded-over sheets of yellow notepaper in his large, boyish,
compulsively neat handwriting, though she prefers his other trick,
taking the receiver off the hook so that, dialing, she will get a busy
signal, repeatedly a busy signal but that way she can tell herself he
is talking on the telephone to someone even if he refuses to talk to
her. And driving the turnpike that afternoon, late, at dusk, where if
something is going to happen to her—frightened as she is, her stomach bad and her brain fractured like glass or ice along fault lines you
would not have guessed were there—it will happen, she thinks wildly,
I'm too young. She thinks, I don't want to die.

When she arrives at the little shingleboard house the door is unlocked but the house is empty, or seems so. Has that feel. That chill
drafty smell. Honey? she calls. Where are you? No one in the front
room and no one in the tiny kitchen and no one in the darkened
bedroom (though the bed has been made, at least the green chenille
spread has been yanked up over the rumpled sheets) and no one in
the spare room that is his study and no one in the dank cubbyhole
of a bathroom where the edges of the windows have been taped to
keep out the wind. So she runs back outside, her hair whipping, tears
in her eyes, and, yes, he's down there on the beach, in the rotted
canvas beach chair they'd found in the tool shed, the Atlantic crashing at his feet, six-foot waves toothed and pocked with white, a crazy
spin to the air and his corpse there, down there, how will she explain
it, on the scrubby debris-littered beach. She cups her hands to her
mouth and screams his name but he seems not to hear, doesn't turn
his head, only when she stands over him does he respond, and then
without much surprise, or emotion: squinting up at her without
seeming to recognize her, his eyes narrowed behind the smudged,

water-specked lenses of his glasses. They stare at each other and finally he says, *You* look like you've seen a ghost, and she laughs and pokes him on the shoulder, Well—have I? and he laughs too, his easy laugh. She tries to keep all reproach out of her voice, saying, Honey, I called you this afternoon but you didn't answer, I was a little worried. . . . Grinning he says, Oh didn't I answer? Yeah? She says, still smiling, Well I was a little worried. You know. Not much but a little. He says, How much? Or how little? She brushes her hair out of her eyes, she's sniffing, trying not to cry, tears of anger and tears of hurt and tears of love, whatever, her counterworld to which (she sees suddenly) no one has access, not even this man. He says in his teacherly, reproving voice, Obviously I didn't hear the phone ring, I was working, or I was outside, out here, probably. Where did you think I was? After a pause she says, Out here. I probably thought you were probably out here.

That's right, sweetheart, he says, staring up at her. Now you've got it.

In bed that night in their drafty bedroom they hug in the old way, at least at first, the first several minutes, laughing, breathless, like children tickling and twining their cold feet together. Then he says, You're spying on me, aren't you?—pinching her buttocks, her breasts. She says, I would never do that. I love you. He says, I love you too but does one proposition exclude the other? She laughs, and says again, I love you. She picks his fingers off her breasts where they hurt. She steels herself waiting for something to happen, as when she waits for him to shut a door hard enough to make the windows and glassware rattle, and he does, or when she waits for his fork to clatter against his plate, and it does. That's what marriage is for, he says, laughing. But after so long a pause she can't remember what they are talking about.

Then he starts again. Playing rough. Tickling. Making her squirm, squeal, kick, struggle, gasp giggling for breath, beg him to stop. You don't trust me do you? he says panting. Spying on me aren't you? She fights him, tries to catch his hands, hair and sweat in her eyes, Of course I trust you, damn you, I *love* you. He says, Why did you marry me if you don't love me? She says, shrieking, But I *do,* I do *love you.* This playing rough, this rough play, sometimes it leads to lovemaking (the kind that hurts) and sometimes it doesn't, Why did you marry me if you don't love me, he demands, rhythmically, fingers digging and poking into her hard, why did you marry me if you don't love me, cunt, why did you marry me if you don't love me, cunt, and she hears a madwoman's screaming laughter, she begs him to stop and finally he does and they lie there sweaty and panting not touching eyes wide in the dark and she says, one final time, a little louder than she intends, But I do.

Anecdote

Her lover is the most conventional of men which is one of the reasons she loves him but today on the street he seems not to recognize her—though he raises his hand politely in response to her greeting, and smiles in response to her smile, and may even have said "Hello" in response to her "Hello." There is a distance of approximately . thirty feet between them as she crosses the street at an intersection and steps up onto the curb and he continues at his usual quick pace without looking back at her.

Of course she is hurt at the time—she is a woman frequently hurt "at the time"—but afterward she concludes that her lover was simply distracted and did not see her; hadn't time to place her in context (since it was in another part of the city that the encounter, or the pseudo-encounter, occurred, not the neighborhood in which they both live); or that he could not acknowledge her ("her" as she appeared on the street, not "her" in the larger sense—that confluence of physical, historical-genetic, spiritual elements that constitute her existence) at that moment for reasons one day to be supplied, should she press for an explanation.

Another possibility is that the man she saw was not her lover but another man who so strongly resembled him as to have been his identical twin brother. Yet another possibility, that the man she saw

was in fact her lover's identical twin brother, whom she has never
met, and whose existence her lover has not acknowledged. Though
the genetic replicant of her lover his twin brother could not have
recognized, or been expected to recognize, her, in any context familiar or unfamiliar.

These several possibilities compete for her attention, now one most
reasonable, now another. She suspects that the incident will simply
evolve, as such things do, into an anecdote; and then, with the passage
of years, into one of those severely abbreviated, highly codified allusions husbands and wives frequently make, often before company, or
before children and other family members who have heard them
numberless times before but out of politeness, or out of actual
bemused affection, tolerate yet another reference.

*There was a day this man passed me on the street without recogniz-
ing me!* she will say as if asking them to believe such a thing, and
everyone will laugh, and *he* will laugh too, embarrassed, protesting,
saying to the company *She knows it wasn't that at all. It was . . .*

Should she press for an explanation.

The Quarrel

Mornings, early, in most weathers, N. jogged around the reservoir, a distance of approximately two miles, while S. made coffee, started breakfast, had his first cigarette of the day sitting in a window alcove of the kitchen reading through *The New York Times;* glancing up repeatedly to follow N.'s progress around the reservoir, knowing now by instinct where N. would appear, at which curve of shore he would disappear, and where, along the sandy strip of shore facing the house, he would again appear, in warm weather in a white T-shirt, through much of the autumn in a red-checked woolen shirt they called his hunter's shirt, jogging easily, in no haste, with no appearance of self-consciousness though he knew that S. was watching, sipping his coffee, smoking his cigarette with a bitter sort of pleasure, thinking, There is my life. What remains of my life.

Once, years ago, his and N.'s love for each other had glowed like phosphorescent fire on the surfaces of their bodies, making them objects of beauty (and perhaps of terror) in others' eyes; now the fire seemed to have retreated . . . invisible, wholly interior, re-siding in the marrow of their bones. They rarely made love now, and they rarely quarreled now, and S., who would be fifty-six years old on his next birthday, N.'s elder by five years, could not have said which he missed more.

It happened that, one wintry morning, when N. returned from jogging, he was attacked by an intruder, a stranger, evidently a would-be thief, hiding in the garage (which was in the ground floor of the old house—the house itself was built into a hill): before N. knew what was happening the man had rushed him, struck him a numbing blow to the side of the head, and N. would have fallen except by instinct he'd grabbed his attacker, shouting for S., for help . . . in the confusion of the moment trying to retain him and not, as of course he should have done, letting him go. There came, however, almost at once, S. from the rear door, shouting too, "Stop! Get away! Who are you! Get away!"—badly frightened, as he would confess afterward, for what if the man had had a gun—and the intruder gave N. a final powerful blow, knocking him against the right front fender of the station wagon, parked there in the sandy-graveled driveway, and turned, and ran up the driveway to the road, and was gone. Like all such astonishing incidents the encounter had happened more swiftly than it could be absorbed, far more swiftly than it would ever be explained, and whether S. had scared off the intruder, and, in a manner of speaking, saved N., or whether the man was preparing to flee anyway, as soon as he freed himself of N.'s inexplicable (and imprudent) grasp, could not be said. Both men were badly agitated: S. helped N. to his feet, N.'s fingers came away from his face covered in blood, "My God what *is* this," he said, amazed, "is this my *blood*?" His attacker had razor-slashed him without either man having seen the razor in his hand.

So N. was treated in the emergency room of the nearest hospital, eight deft stitches, a stinging sort of pain, and afterward, at police headquarters, police officers questioned N. and S. separately—which was, evidently, standard police procedure: N. carefully described his attacker as a "light-skinned black" in his late twenties, weighing approximately two hundred pounds, about six feet, two inches tall, with a narrow moustache, deep-set bloodshot eyes "like a dog's," wearing a soiled sheepskin jacket, work trousers, and a dark green wool-knit cap pulled down low on his forehead; S. carefully described the man as Caucasian, with a sallow, coarse, "possibly pitted" skin, between thirty and thirty-five years old, weighing approximately one hundred seventy or eighty pounds, wearing a nondescript jacket, and jeans, and a navy blue wool-knit cap pulled down low on his forehead. N. described the man's voice as low and guttural while S. was positive the man had not spoken once, at least in his hearing . . . but then of course he'd been so excited, and had been shouting himself, it was impossible to remember.

Since the men's descriptions of N.'s attacker were so different, the police decided against having a composite drawing attempted, nor was there much point in their considering photographs of possible suspects, though they did so, doggedly, stubbornly, for the remainder of the morning, peering at the photostatted images of men who might reasonably be identified as light-skinned blacks or sallow-skinned Caucasians, but the effort seemed futile, the faces began to blur and jumble, and though they tried to maintain an air of absolute civility with each other, N. said, at last, in an embittered voice, "You're doing this to humiliate me, aren't you?—contradicting every damn thing I *saw*." S. stared at him, astonished, and N. added, "Every damn thing I saw with my own eyes." S. said, "To humiliate you? But why? What on earth do you mean?" and suddenly they were quarreling, quietly, yet wildly, not minding that one of the police detectives was listening, or, if minding, if marginally aware of the fact, unable to stop, N.'s heavy face appearing heavier with blood, darkening, and his eyes angrily bright, S.'s heart beating hard, fast, erratic. One said, "I got a good close look at the man and I know what I saw," and the other said, "*I* got a perfectly good look at him and *I* know what I saw," and added, in a spiteful whisper, "Don't be ridiculous, please: you are making yourself ridiculous in public." The other said, staring, "I can't believe you would do this to me, *you!* do this to *me!*" and the other shot back, "*I* can't believe you would do this to *me!*" as the youngish police officer tried not too obviously to

listen, embarrassed, or perhaps amused, and afterward, ah afterward
he would entertain his buddies by mimicking in high-pitched breathless voices N. and S.'s quarrel which like a brushfire flared up as if
from a single spark and ran and ran, wild, terrible, searing, until at
last it burned itself out and S. was wiping his mouth with a handker-
chief, badly trembling, and N. had slammed shut his book of photostatted pictures saying he'd come back another time, maybe another
time would be best, this wasn't a good time right now, he didn't think.
On their way out of the police station S. tried to soothe things over
with a joke, asking one of the detectives if "this sort of thing happens
often," and he and N. saw the man think hard, think frowningly hard,
wondering what exactly S. meant by "this sort of thing"—the dis-
crepancy in the descriptions of the wanted man, or the subsequent
quarrel—before he answered, politely, perhaps condescendingly,
"All the time, yes sure it happens all the time, eyewitnesses are never
reliable," smiling at S. and N. as if to reassure them, "—almost never
reliable."

"How could you do that to me, —I mean, simply, how could you."
    "How could you do that to *me*? And quarreling in front of—"
    "Which you began."
    "Which *you* began. With such evident, such—palpable—
pleasure."
    "The pleasure was all yours."
    "There was no pleasure! It was *yours.*"
    "And in front of—"
    "That isn't how I remember it!"
    "That isn't how I remember it!"

They returned to the splendid century-old five-gabled brown-shingled
house overlooking the reservoir, S. driving the station wagon, N.
furious and silent beside him, compulsively touching the bandage on

his cheek, until, unable to contain himself, S. whispered, "Please *don't.*" For the remainder of that very long day the men were icily civil with each other, for the remainder of that week they were stiff, cautious, circumspect, knowing that the terrible quarrel still smoldered underground like a peat fire and they dared not stir it, provoke it, give it air, for had not S. seen the loathing in N.'s face, there in the police station? and had not N. seen the mockery in S.'s face, like a child grimacing into a mirror?—even as both men well knew that the outburst of a mere moment, particularly in such strained, heightened circumstances, does not really count. Several times S. prepared to say, in a little speech, "You must realize don't you that I hurt a number of people badly for your sake," but could not bring himself to utter the first syllable, and several times N. prepared to say, in the tone he'd used during those years when, intermittently, he had choreographed difficult dance sequences for a New York City troupe, sometimes with conspicuous success, sometimes not, and the dancers, some of whom were very young, had needed not merely to hear but to understand, "You must realize that *life is a serious affair.* "

And weeks passed. And months. And then it was six months, and they never heard any longer from the police, about whom they joked, bitterly, but always cautiously: how ineffectual they'd been about "that thing that had happened back in November," how little you can rely upon them really. At least in such minor matters. And in time the hairbreadth of a scar on N.'s right cheek came to seem hardly more than a curious sort of downward crease in the skin (which was beginning rather more seriously to crease along other, horizontal fault lines) about which they never spoke. And then, one spring evening, when the men were entertaining friends at dinner, S. told of the incident—"our mysterious little adventure"—but his delivery was impeccably light, his tone light, as a popular lecturer at the small liberal arts college at which he'd taught for the past twenty years (S.'s specialty was twentieth-century Europe "post- and prewar") he knew how crucial it was to keep one's tone light, and the thing that had happened back in November, the thing in the driveway, the thing between the two men that had frightened them so, became, now, an anecdote . . . a tale meant to amuse . . . its upshot being not that he and N. had disagreed so violently nor even that N. had been permanently scarred (no mention was made of the scar) but that the police, for all their seeming professionalism, had done so remarkably little. Had anything been taken from the garage or the house, the men were asked, and the answer was no, nothing, that was the puzzle, the mystery, why had the man been there and what had he intended, the entire episode, S. concluded, was inexplicable, sui generis, but of course they kept their doors and windows locked at all times now even during the day even when they were both home, and so on and so forth, and eventually the conversation shifted to other crimes in the area, solved or unsolved, comical or serious or frankly tragic: the rape of an eleven-year-old girl in the next township; the death, by cardiac arrest, of an elderly widow whom some of the company knew, when a never apprehended burglar had broken into her house in the middle of the night.

So the episode became, in a sense, public; published. And now the men were free to allude to it if they wished, though always in anecdotal terms, with wry expressions, the central theme, indeed the only theme, being police incompetence and unreliability. And the years passed, and the years. And never did they risk another scene like that terrible scene in the police station. And they never wept, at least to each other's knowledge. And they never quarreled again.

Pinch

She must have swallowed a tiny pit, or a thorn, that made its way into the fatty tissue of her left breast and would not budge. Day after day, during the night, stealthily, she felt it there—pinching the flesh until it ached.

She made her way to the radiology department of the hospital, bearing a green slip. A young nurse led her to the women's gowning room which had a close, tropical smell. There, she undressed quickly with a fear that someone would interrupt her. She put on a green smock, many times too large for her, open at the back, that tied at the nape of the neck but flapped open as she walked.

Led by the nurse to the X-ray room she saw how, in the corridor, many eyes followed her.

The X-ray room was windowless and air-conditioned. In it, a single mammoth machine rose to the ceiling. She stood staring at it as the nurse helped her disrobe, her breasts like drooping melons, sallow and blue-veined. The nipples looked worn, cracked, as if they had been sucked and gnawed numberless times, which was not the case. "You may find the machine cold at first," the nurse said. It was a warning couched in kindness. "It may pinch a little."

Though she was a tall woman she stood on a stool so that the nurse could fit her breast into the clamp. It had to be held tight, slightly flattened; the nurse had difficulty adjusting it and had to try several times. She told the woman to lean forward, no, to lean forward and to the side, like this, as if she were resting, relaxed, her armpit snug against a bar. The bar was cold. The clamp hurt her breast. "It may pinch a little," the nurse said again, tightening the clamp so that the woman bit her lip but did not cry out as she believed she was expected to do.

The nurse hid herself adroitly behind a shield. A sudden whirring noise filled the room as the machine came to life and the woman stood on the stool with her eyes closed.

"Now, the other side," said the nurse brightly.

The breast was unclamped and the other breast inserted. Again the woman leaned forward and to the side, trying to relax, her armpit pressed against a bar. The procedure was done twice over and when it was finished the nurse left the room with the X-ray film and the woman was allowed to sit, weak, shivering, at the end of an examining table with stirrups. Both her breasts were sore and she imagined that her left nipple had begun to bleed but she did not examine it closely. She had been told to put the green smock back on; with unsteady fingers she tied the strings at the nape of her neck.

After forty minutes a doctor came to examine her. The nurse returned with the X-ray photographs which he examined for some time, frowning. The doctor was a short, dapper, nearly bald man: a stranger: the woman had never seen him before and avoided his eyes now. She was told his name but did not hear it.

He asked her to disrobe and she did so, but slowly. The doctor's fingers were skillful and deft but her breasts were already sore from the machine and as he prodded and squeezed and manipulated and flattened her flesh the woman bit her lip to keep from crying out. The doctor then asked her to lie back on the examining table, which she did, though slowly, as if the request were an unnatural one. Tears ran out of the corners of the woman's eyes when her head came to rest on the flat leather pillow.

Now the doctor stands over her kneading her breasts vigorously.

He stands with his head inclined as if he is listening for something the woman can't hear. He asks her questions, her voice replies intelligently, but in a neutral tone, as if from a distance. She might be speaking over the telephone. She is not crying now and there is really no evidence that she has been crying, if she has been crying.

The doctor has gone away, the woman and the nurse are left alone together in the X-ray room. It has become difficult for the woman to hear voices over the hum of the air conditioning but she understands that more X-rays are required and she intends to obey. She sees for the first time that the nurse is quite pretty, with a plump flushed face, plump reddened lips. The nurse helps her step up onto the stool, and helps fit her breast into the clamp. "This may pinch a little," the nurse says, licking her pretty lips.

Secret

She is thinking that, though he basks in her adoration, in his belief that her dependence upon him is absolute, and therefore craven, she really loathes him and hopes for harm, hurt, sorrow, even horror to befall him. She is thinking that, though he believes she is stupidly faithful to him despite his unfaithfulness to her—a sign, in his imagination, of her female ("feminine") weakness—she has in mind the project of outliving him, simply.

Why otherwise does her face light up in his presence? Why her eyes shining like a young girl's? Why repay sarcasm with sweetness, irritability with gentleness, coarseness with delicacy, subtlety, "art"? A few of his older friends have guessed at her secret, it's true, but she gives no indication of guessing they've guessed and of course they can't—will never—know. Already she is settling into a comfortable chair at his bedside, it's morning in some nameless white place and he's blind perhaps or nearly, deaf, or nearly, the thing inhabiting him has drained away his strength and his "manhood" or was it a stroke that fell upon him indeed like a stroke of an ax she didn't wield, she can't be held to blame humming under her breath as she does needlepoint or reads a book or busies herself sorting through the morning's mail he'll continue to receive even after his death—letters from strangers, letters from old friends, begging letters, homage letters,

letters from those who hope, too late, to meet him and to attach their empty lives to his with the intention of arousing his need for their adoration and burrowing into his life, perhaps even to marry him, outlive him, become his widow. Too late.

Ace

A gang of overgrown boys, aged eighteen to twenty-five, has taken over the northeast corner of our park again this summer. Early evenings they start arriving, hang out until the park closes at midnight. Nothing to do but get high on beer and dope, the police leave them alone as long as they mind their own business, don't hassle people too much. Now and then there's fighting but nothing serious—nobody shot or stabbed.

Of course no girl or woman in her right mind would go anywhere near them, if she didn't have a boyfriend there.

Ace is the leader, a big boy in his twenties with a mean baby-face, pouty mouth, and cheeks so red they look fresh-slapped, sly little steely eyes curling up at the corners like he's laughing or getting ready to laugh. He's six foot two weighing maybe two hundred twenty pounds—lifts weights at the gym—but there's some loose flabby flesh around his middle, straining against his belt. He goes bare-chested in the heat, likes to sweat in the open air, muscles bunched and gleaming, and he can show off his weird tattoos—ace of spades on his right bicep, inky-black octopus on his left. Long shaggy hair the color of dirty sand and he wears a red sweatband for looks.

Nobody notices anything special about a car circling the park, lots of traffic on summer nights and nobody's watching then there's this popping noise like a firecracker and right away Ace screams and claps his hand to his eye and it's streaming blood—what the hell? Did somebody shoot him? His buddies just freeze not knowing what to do. There's a long terrible minute when everybody stands there staring at Ace not knowing what to do—then the boys run and duck for cover, scattering like pigeons. And Ace is left alone standing there, crouched, his hand to his left eye screaming, Help, Jesus, hey, help, my eye— Standing there crouched at the knee like he's waiting for a second shot to finish him off.

The bullet must have come at an angle, skimmed the side of Ace's face, otherwise he'd be flat-out dead lying in the scrubby grass. He's panicked though, breathing loud through his mouth saying, O Jesus, O Jesus, and after a minute people start yelling, word's out there's been a shooting and somebody's hurt. Ace wheels around like he's been hit again but it's only to get away, suddenly he's walking fast stooped over dripping blood, could be he's embarrassed, doesn't want people to see him, red headband and tattoos, and now he's dripping blood down his big beefy forearm, in a hurry to get home.

Some young girls have started screaming. Nobody knows what has happened for sure and where Ace is headed people clear out of his way. There's blood running down his chest, soaking into his jeans, splashing onto the sidewalk. His friends are scared following along after him asking where he's going, is he going to the hospital, but Ace glares up out of his one good eye like a crazy man, saying, Get the fuck away! Don't touch me! and nobody wants to come near.

On the street the cops stop him and there's a call put in for an ambulance. Ace stands there dazed and shamed and the cops ask him questions as if he's to blame for what happened, was he in a fight, where's he coming from, is that a bullet wound?—all the while a crowd's gathering, excitement in the air you can feel. It's an August night, late, eighty-nine degrees and no breeze. The crowd is all strangers, Ace's friends have disappeared. he'd beg the cops to let him go but his heart is beating so hard he can't get his breath. Starts swaying like a drunk man, his knees so weak the cops have to steady him. They can smell the panic sweat on him, running in rivulets down his sides.

In the ambulance he's held in place and a black orderly tells him he's O.K., he's going to be O.K., goin' to be at the hospital in two minutes flat. He talks to Ace the way you'd talk to a small child, or an animal. They give him some quick first aid trying to stop the bleeding but Ace can't control himself can't hold still, he's crazy with fear, his heart gives a half-dozen kicks then it's off and going—like a drum tattoo right in his chest. The ambulance is tearing along the street, siren going, Ace says O God O God O God his terrible heartbeat carrying him away.

He's never been in a hospital in his life—knows he's going to die there.

Then he's being hauled out of the ambulance. Stumbling through automatic-eye doors not knowing where he is. Jaws so tight he could grind his teeth away and he can't get his breath and he's ashamed how people are looking at him, right there in the lights in the hallway people staring at his face like they'd never seen anything so terrible. He can't keep up with the attendants, knees buckling and his heart beating so hard but they don't notice, trying to make him walk faster, Come on man they're saying, you ain't hurt that bad, Ace just can't keep up and he'd fall if they weren't gripping him under the arms then he's in the emergency room and lying on a table, filmy white curtains yanked closed around him and there's a doctor, two nurses, What seems to be the trouble here the doctor asks squinting at Ace through his glasses, takes away the bloody gauze and doesn't flinch at what he sees. He warns Ace to lie still, he sounds tired and annoyed as if Ace is to blame, how did this happen he asks but doesn't wait for any answer and Ace lies there stiff and shivering with fear clutching at the underside of the table so hard his nails are digging through the tissue-paper covering into the vinyl, he can't see out of his left eye, nothing there but pain, pain throbbing and pounding everywhere in his head and the nurses—are there two? three?—look down at him with sympathy he thinks, with pity he thinks, they're attending to him, touching him, nobody has ever touched him so tenderly in all his life Ace thinks and how shamed he is hauled in here like this flat on his back like this bleeding like a stuck pig and sweating bare-chested and his big gut exposed quivering there in the light for everybody to see—

The doctor puts eight stitches in Ace's forehead, tells him he's damned lucky he didn't lose his eye, the bullet missed it by about two inches and it's going to be swollen and blackened for a while, next time you might not be so lucky he says but Ace doesn't catch this, his heart's going so hard. They wrap gauze around his head tight then hook him up to a machine to monitor his heartbeat, the doctor's whistling under his breath like he's surprised, lays the flat of his hand against Ace's chest to feel the weird loud rocking beat. Ace is broken out in sweat but it's cold clammy sick sweat, he knows he's going to die. The machine is going bleep-bleep-bleep high-pitched and fast and how fast can it go before his heart bursts?—he sees the nurses looking down at him, one of the nurses just staring at him, Don't let me die Ace wants to beg but he'd be too ashamed. The doctor is listening to Ace's heartbeat with his stethoscope, asks does he have any pain in his chest, has he ever had an attack like this before, Ace whispers no but too soft to be heard, all the blood has drained from his face and his skin is dead-white, mouth gone slack like a fish's and toes like ice where Death is creeping up his feet: he can feel it.

The heart isn't Ace's heart but just something inside him gone angry and mean pounding like a hammer pounding pounding pounding against his ribs making his body rock so he's panicked suddenly and wants to get loose, tries to push his way off the table—he isn't thinking but if he could think he'd say he wanted to leave behind what's happening to him here as if it was only happening in the emergency room, there on that table. But they don't let him go. There's an outcry in the place and two orderlies hold him down and he gives up, all the strength drained out of him and he gives up, there's no need to strap him down the way they do, he's finished.

They hook him up to the heart monitor again and the terrible high-pitched bleeping starts again and he lies there shamed knowing he's going to die he's forgotten about the gunshot, his eye, who did it and was it on purpose meant for him and how can he get revenge, he's forgotten all that covered in sick clammy sweat his nipples puckered and the kinky hairs on his chest wet, even his belly button showing exposed from the struggle and how silly and sad his tattoos must look under these lights where they were never meant to be seen.

One of the nurses sinks a long needle in his arm, and there's another needle in the soft thin flesh of the back of his hand, takes him by surprise, they've got a tube in there, and something coming in hot and stinging dripping into his vein the doctor's telling him something he can't follow, This is to bring the heartbeat down the doctor says, just a tachycardia attack and it isn't fatal try to relax but Ace knows he's going to die, he can feel Death creeping up his feet up his legs like stepping out into cold water and suddenly he's so tired he can't lift his head, couldn't get up from the table if they unstrapped him. And he dies—it's that easy.

Like slipping off into the water, pushing out, letting the water take you. It's that easy.

They're asking Ace if he saw who shot him and Ace says, Naw, didn't see nobody. They ask does he have enemies and he says, Naw, no more than anybody else. They ask can he think of anybody who might have wanted to shoot him and he says, embarrassed, looking down at the floor with his one good eye, Naw, can't think of nobody right now. So they let him go.

Next night Ace is back in the park out of pride but there's a feeling to him he isn't real or isn't the same person he'd been. One eye bandaged shut and everything looks flat, people staring at him like he's a freak, wanting to know What about the eye and Ace shrugs and tells them he's O.K., the bullet just got his forehead. Everybody wants to speculate who fired the shot, whose car it was, but Ace stands sullen and quiet thinking his own thoughts. Say he'd been standing just a little to one side the bullet would have got him square in the forehead or plowed right into his eye, killed him dead, it's something to think about and he tries to keep it in mind so he'll feel good. But he doesn't feel good. He doesn't feel like he'd ever felt before. His secret is something that happened to him in the hospital he can't remember except to know it happened and it happened to him. And he's in a mean mood his head half-bandaged like a mummy, weird-looking in the dark, picking up on how people look at him and say things behind his back calling him Ace which goes through him like a razor because it's a punk name and not really his.

Mostly it's O.K. He hides how he feels. He's got a sense of humor. He doesn't mind them clowning around pretending they hear gun-shots and got to duck for cover, nobody's going to remember it for long, except once Ace stops laughing and backhands this guy in the belly, low below the belt, says in his old jeering voice, What do you know?—you don't know shit.

Heartland

She has driven one thousand miles into the heartland of the country to visit her parents, whom she hasn't seen in a very long time, and within an hour she wonders if she has made a mistake—there is an atmosphere of strain in the household and neither of her parents seems overjoyed to see her though they have gone through the customary ritual of embraces, kisses, protracted and reiterated greetings, such questions as How *are* you? and such remarks as How good you look! as they smile at one another so hard it hurts. It might almost be that she has walked into the wrong house except this *is* the house, and these *are* her parents, about whom she has brooded for so long knowing that they love her as their only child and are hurt that she so rarely comes to visit. Over the telephone her mother is careful to say, I realize you're busy, dear—you have a very demanding job, and her father will say, Don't worry about us! The old gal and I are doing fine! Love ya!

This time, however, when she telephoned announcing her visit her mother sounded distracted and didn't seem to recognize her voice at first perhaps because, in the background, a television set was turned up unnaturally high. Loud voices punctuated by laughter and swells of music and her mother didn't say, Excuse me—let me turn this down, but spoke over the noise, which was disconcerting. Her father wasn't there, or wasn't able to come to the telephone, so they made their plans hurriedly, when she'd arrive, how long she'd stay, what the special things were she might do with them and for them while she was there, and still her mother sounded vague and not at all warm and animated as she usually was so she asked, Is something wrong, Mother? Is one of you not feeling well? and her mother said curtly, Of course not, it's just that you called at an awkward time.

Now she's here and she understands that she has come, too, at an awkward time. Though why, what's wrong, she can't determine.

Her mother, who has never used cosmetics, is heavily made-up, bright lipstick, spots of rouge on her cheeks, her hair no longer a dull yellowish gray but a canary yellow permed in tight little curls like wire. Her father, who is a retired post office employee, has a new pair of false teeth, very white, ceramic, that glisten wetly when he smiles and he is in the habit now of smiling often, which she doesn't remember. Her father was always the brooder of the family and in her innocent anecdotizing of her past she'll attribute her own predilection for brooding to the genes she has inherited "from his side of the family" as if this were the House of Atreus. Now her father is a hearty laughing youngish-old man with a hairpiece so cleverly woven into his own scanty hair she can scarcely tell which is which. And his voice is higher-pitched than she remembers. Well! he says repeatedly. Well!—rubbing his hands together energetically, his cheeks bunching in smiles—how *are* ya! Damn good to *see* ya! Your mother and I *miss* ya—ya *know* that!

Her mother leads her upstairs weakly apologizing for the "condition" her old room is in, and she's shocked to enter it and see that it isn't her old room, her girlhood room, any longer, but a room used for storage, a clutter-room, boxes, cartons, odd items of furniture, a headless dressmaker's dummy, an antiquated manual typewriter on the floor, the keys so thick with dust their letters are obscured. She doesn't remember the typewriter. She doesn't remember her room quite so cramped and was there only one window?—in her memory the room was flooded with light. But there is her bed, and there, behind a propped-up card table, her old bureau with the mirror on the back that could be moved on its hinges. As a child she'd swing it upward and watch her face disappear out the bottom like something draining out of a tub, or she'd swing it downward and her face flew out the top. The mirror too is coated with dust and in it her mother's and her faces are so dimly reflected they're nothing but animated blurs. They might be the same face duplicated except her mother's red lips and florid cheeks stand out.

Her mother is saying that if she'd had time to get things ready, if she'd been feeling stronger, if the visit hadn't been "tossed into their laps like this . . ." and she replies, hurt, that she doesn't have to stay here she can stay at a motel and her mother says defensively, No, no, what kind of hospitality is that! What would people say!—so she's obliged to sleep in that bed and her migraine headache begins and coming back downstairs where her father is pacing restlessly and whistling in the kitchen she feels as if someone has hit her over the head with a sledgehammer because there's no getting out of this is there? Her parents confer in low urgent voices in the kitchen as she pretends to study some framed photographs on a table in the living room and through the doorway she can see slantwise her father nodding brusquely not smiling now, his expression coarse and mean, she understands they're saying to each other, There's no getting out of this is there? and, Why did she come when nobody invited her?

At dinner, which they eat in the kitchen on plastic placemats with the overhead light shining fiercely down, her parents chide each other for things they've done recently or failed to do, for instance her father is naughty about taking his blood pressure pills every morning and her mother is "much worse" about sticking to her diet. They drift into a picky lackluster quarrel about when she last came home to visit (two years? three years? five?) and she's teary-eyed from the migraine but trying to keep her composure recalling visits home from college when she'd proudly showed them her papers with her professors' comments in red ink—Brilliant! Remarkable insight! *Very* skillfully organized!—and each of them made an attempt to read what she'd written, her father brooding over some of her phrases and allusions because he couldn't understand them and needed her to explain, her mother just reading with a small fixed smile saying sighing afterward, Well—it's all beyond *me* but I think it's *wonderful.* This visit, it's painfully conspicuous, their lack of interest in her career, her exciting urban life a thousand miles away, by degrees she gathers from her mother's perfunctory questions that they don't really know what her work, these days, *is,* and when she tries to explain their eyes glaze over and her father's eyelids droop. He rises from his chair with a happy smile—It's all beyond *me!*

She says she'll take care of the dishes assuming she and her mother will do them together as always but her mother says, Good, I can use some rest, I've been on my feet all day, and she and the father watch television while the daughter cleans up the mess in the kitchen which takes her some time—out of martyrdom she scrubs the counters with steel wool, they're shockingly grimy, and the sink is virtually covered with a film of grease so she scours that too, then she's on her hands and knees sponging up some of the worst spots on the linoleum floor while in the other room television noises are loud and festive and her parents not only laugh at whatever it is they're watching but exclaim now and then, her father particularly, Hey! Chree—ist! Look at *that!*

When she joins them they glance up at her as if they don't at first recognize her then there's a long hour, a very long hour, the three of them watching a police comedy, and then it's 11:00 P.M. and time for a snack in the kitchen so she joins them since there's nothing else to do, stuffing their faces with butterscotch-ripple ice cream and Oreo cookies and her mother is wearing a shiny jade-green rayon robe with a sash tied tight at her waist and her father is wearing just an undershirt and trousers and there's a flirty sort of banter between them, her mother poking her father in what she calls his "beer gut" and her father poking her mother in what he calls her "big bosom" and she's thinking they should be ashamed of themselves at their ages even as, smiling, embarrassed, she tries to fall in with their mood—joking that

her father looks "twenty years younger" than the last time she saw
him, and her mother's a "glamour girl," and they like that, or give
that impression.

Saying good night her parents lean into each other, her father's arm
around her mother's waist and her mother's canary-bright head co-
quettishly tilted. See ya at breakfast! says her father with his glistening smile and now she's in bed in that room smelling of dust and old
clothes and she can hear from her parents' room down the hall the
sounds of lovemaking punctuated by voices and even laughter,
though she isn't sure that it's real because her parents have a second
television set in their bedroom and very likely they've turned it on.

Maximum Security

The State Correctional Facility for Men, maximum security, was on the far side of the river in an old neighborhood of factories, warehouses, abandoned derelict buildings. It was in a part of the city she never visited and when she drove her car along the expressway she found herself staring at the prison walls without knowing at first what she saw. Sometimes she had to roll her car window up tight against a pungent smell as of slightly overripe oranges but the smell came from a chemical factory close by and had nothing to do with the prison.

One February morning she was taken on a tour through the prison in the company of several other interested parties. A criminologist from the state university, two social workers, an administrator from the public advocate's office. The tour was conducted by an officer from the State Department of Correction; it began at 9:00 A.M. and ended after 11:00 A.M. She had foreseen that the visit would be exhausting and depressing but she was not prepared for her immediate sense of panicked déjà vu as soon as the first of numerous gates locked in place behind her.

There were a half-dozen separate checkpoints going in. Gates, doors, camera-eyes, guards in pale blue uniforms. You will of course not be addressing any of the inmates directly, the officer said. He had coarse sandy hair in a fringe around a smooth scalp, his eyebrows were thickly tufted, he smiled and frowned a good deal as he spoke, and generally looked over the heads of the visitors. Around his waist, on his left side, he was wearing a pistol with a polished wooden handle strapped into a smart black-gleaming leather holster.

The prisoners were observed without incident through wire-enforced plate-glass windows. They appeared to be quite ordinary men though a number were big, ponderous, solid as elephants, with faces too that seemed to be composed of muscle. They sat at long narrow tables, or stood motionless, or walked about in lazy scattered groups in an area starkly illuminated by fluorescent lights. A double tier of cells to the rear, no windows visible. Armed robbery, murder, car theft, wife and child beating, drug dealing, and so forth, the officer was saying in an affable toneless voice. Here they're under strict surveillance and they know it. They don't like surprises, breaks in the routine. They get upset easy. For instance if the hot water's out and the schedule has to be rearranged.

What they mainly think about, the officer said, is parole.

No they don't think much about the past, he said. To their way of thinking—I am referring to your average inmate—the past is something that is over with. They look to the future now.

Amid the prisoners there was here and there a white face, startlingly pale. She asked the officer why most of the prisoners they saw were black and the officer said, as if he'd been asked the question many times before, It's the way the system works out, ma'am.

They walked on, they observed another cell block, and another, and the officer was saying, Men hate being locked up. Women don't mind it the same way, it's more like what they're used to—that's one theory. Also in the prison system they're protected as long as they stay in. They're protected from the men.

There was a vibrating hum in the distance like a waterfall. Dull rumbling thunder. Anger, she thought. Rage. In fact it was the ventilating system. Any questions? the officer asked.

Raindrops large as grapes splashed onto the graveled roof as they were led across to observe the outdoor volleyball court and the yard. She lifted her face to the rain, wondered if she was crying, felt again that profound conviction of déjà vu: I have been here before. This is happiness, she thought. The raindrops on the very edge of freezing to sleet.

She had stopped listening to the officer's voice and to the intelligent thoughtful questions of the other visitors. In the distance, away from the city, the horizon was like steam in orange-tinted pockets or clots dissolving into the sky. The river was the hue of stainless steel cutlery. Traffic on the expressway, slow-moving, ceaseless. It gave her great comfort to see the prison walls at last from the inside yet to look over them too. To your right, the officer said, you'll observe the yard. Inmates are allotted two hours a day under ordinary circumstances. Sometimes there's organized sports but most of them just like to stand around, get some fresh air. They're mostly waiting for the next meal, he said.

The Assignation

At the rear of the duplex apartment overlooking the alley, shades negligently drawn and a faint light burning, she's a silhouette moving from window to window then suddenly visible in her underwear, white skin, luminous white skin, arms lifted, yawning.

She was wakened from her groggy daytime sleep by a noise in the alley or in the adjacent apartment where the television is often turned up high because there's a woman who lives alone there, and is lonely. Lying for a while in the unmade bed amid the lazy sheets her heart pounding in dread, worry, excitement. Is someone there? she calls. Knowing no one will answer.

It's mid-December. Just past 5:00 P.M. but dark as night. She lay down a couple of hours ago not intending to sleep then of course she did sleep, like slipping off the edge of something, you don't want to let go and then you do. Wakened by some noise she didn't exactly hear like seeing something out of the corner of your eye you don't exactly see. Know who that is?—that's Baby, her father said squatting beside her pointing to the angel at the very top of the Christmas tree, white satin skirt, round bland face, gilt cardboard halo. They called her Baby then, she hadn't her real name yet. A long time ago and probably he'd been drinking and she never thinks of him except slantwise, an old worn-smooth thought that's even comforting now, hasn't, now, the power to hurt. In the bedsheets she lies unmoving not daring to move for a long time.

She switches on a light yawning and stumbling her hair in her face and her pulsebeat still fast which means something is going to happen and she doesn't know what except it's something she wants to happen, or thinks she wants. Turns on the radio to the usual station, where there's music twenty-four hours a day. She finds her cigarettes and lighter in the things piled on the bureau then goes out into the kitchen not troubling to switch on the light, the light from the opened refrigerator is enough, she takes out a can of beer, opens it, swallows a mouthful or two then sets it back inside. Returns to the bedroom cigarette in hand walking hard on her bare feet, her heels. The shades in this room are crooked not quite meeting the windowsills or maybe they're broken and she should see about getting them repaired but that's the kind of thing, she says, you don't get around to doing, you know, you just think of when you're actually looking at it then other times you forget. Like there's people you're crazy about when you're with them and you know they like you too but then, if you're not with them, if you're not in the room with them, you sort of forget each other and that's a shame I mean it's a goddamned shame but it doesn't mean anything. It's just how things are.

———————————⊱✦⊰———————————

This is a neighborhood of duplexes and row houses and old single-family houses converted to apartments. Row after row in the dripping rain. Cars parked at the curbs, windows lit, a smell of wood smoke, creosote. The center is everywhere and the circumference nowhere which is why this place has no name. Or, named, cannot be remem-

bered even by its inhabitants once they pass on, as many, or all, do.
She uses the toilet without troubling to close the door, turns on the
shower inside the stained Plexiglas stall, lets the water run until it's
steaming which is the way she likes it, she's warm-blooded, hopeful,
a little nervous about tonight but excited too, careful to wrap her long
hair in a towel so it won't get wet—the elastic band in her shower
cap has gone slack and she should buy a new one, it's no trouble to
buy a new one, Woolworth's, the drugstore, but she won't remember
unless she writes it down. In the shower she soaps her body slowly
and languorously, her belly, her breasts, her armpits, her thighs so
fleshy and warm, between her thighs the scratchy pubic hair, and her
legs, her feet, between her toes, where, in summer, there's likely to
be a gritty film of dirt, now there's nothing, or nearly—she showers
often, if not once a day at least several times a week. She loves
standing beneath the shower her eyes shut in the sheer joy of it
smiling into the streaming water as hot as she can bear, how wonderful here, how safe here, you want it never to end. The telephone
receiver is off the hook so she doesn't have to worry about that or even
think about that, not now and not here, it has been off the hook since
early afternoon since before she lay down for her nap though she
hadn't really meant to sleep just to lie down for a while to put her
thoughts in order about the night before, the night maybe to come,
before last night and beyond tonight it's all vague and formless like
a lit place where the farther you get from the center of radiance
the more shadowy and vague objects become until finally there's nothing there at all and you're staring into the dark seeing nothing.
So she loves the hot water springing from the nozzle, the steam filling
up the bathroom, eyes shut not seeing the tile with its arabesques of
cracks and fractures, the inside of the shower stall splotched with
grime, not seeing and not wanting to see, that would only break
the mood.

What you do and want to do. Again and again. Without ever stop-
ping. Or, if you stop, it's only to recover, to begin again—if it has the

feel of killing it isn't, always. It's in your control but not, in a sense, in *your* control since, at such times, in the exigencies of such times, who precisely are *you?*—and *why?* And, not extraneous here, *who is a witness?*

She dries herself slowly, taking as always, in the steamy aftermath of the shower, her slow time. Wrapped in the big blue bath towel with the loose threads. Slow movements to keep back the race of her pulse because she's beginning to be excited about what's to come not knowing precisely what it will be only that it will be different from the previous night as that night was different from the night previous to it and even when nothing happens there is always the possibility that something might have happened or had in fact nearly happened and was by the sheerest chance or accident deflected. You have to take your chances, she says, can't just bury your head in the sand for Christ's sake.

She rubs her body with hand lotion, breasts, buttocks and thighs, belly, legs. She's hypnotized by the feel, the weight, of so much heated fleshy flesh—its inertness, otherness. Is this me or am I inside it is a thought she doesn't, probably, think, wiping away steam from the mirror to observe herself critically, the flushed face, eyes mascara-smudged on the lower lid, the perfect nose a lover cracked across the bridge with a backhanded blow some years ago but you can't tell, or almost can't tell, there's anything the slightest wrong. She rinses her face in cold water to close the pores then rubs in moisturizer stroking upward carefully from the chin then puts on makeup in slow amorous strokes carefully as if she is painting a mask, a gluey puttylike substance shaken from a bottle, powder applied on top of that with a stained powder puff and then the eyes, a tiny mascara brush, inky-black mascara stiffening the eyelashes like spiders' legs then the eyebrows darkened with an eyebrow pencil then the mouth.

Now in her underwear, black bra, beige underpants, she goes out into the kitchen again and takes the can of beer out of the refrigerator and brings it back into the bedroom, lights another cigarette smoking it while she dresses with the same slow studied deliberate motions with which she dried herself, a slowness inside which there is something beating quick and impatient. A telephone rings but it's the telephone in the apartment next door but still she pauses momentarily, listens, staring toward the wall, then resumes dressing again takes another swallow of beer examines herself frowning in the full-length mirror on the closet door not liking, or is it liking, what she sees. Know who that is?—that's Baby.

In the kitchen she heats up some coffee at the stove and drinks it standing at the sink too restless to sit down. The radio is playing loud rock music of a few years back, a song so familiar she doesn't have to listen to feel the beat. She touches her hair several times as if not knowing what she does, stares at her shadowy reflection in the window above the sink, the curly kinky hair, the savage painted-on mouth. Does she see someone else there and if so whom?—stubbing her cigarette out in an ashtray. She adds the coffee cup to the dishes in the sink from that morning or from the previous day, soaking in cold grayish water, then returns to the bedroom, moving more quickly now. She puts on a pair of earrings, inclining her head first to one side, then to the other, as she slips the tiny wires through the tiny holes in her ears. She puts on several bracelets, several rings. The bedside clock with its greeny luminous dials and stark open frank affable face reads 6:20.

She turns the radio off. Sits on the bed to make a telephone call, lights up another cigarette. No answer when she dials so she tries again and still no answer so she pushes the phone away, the receiver is on the hook now, she goes into the bathroom to check her makeup and hair, switches off the light and finds her purse in the bedroom and hurries to the front of the apartment to the closet where she takes out her boots—knee-high leather or simulated leather boots with a two-inch heel—and puts them on. And her coat—black cloth with a dyed rabbit collar that crests glamorously about her face and hair. This is a coat, she likes to say, I paid for myself. Paid for in cash.

Except for the light in the bedroom the apartment is darkened, and silent. She leaves another light burning by the front door. Steps outside shivering in anticipation or is it with the cold, stands for several contemplative seconds on the front stoop staring out toward the street into the darkness beyond the street where, eventually, I am waiting.

Fin de Siècle

Doc Junius was this disgustingly obese old guy eighty-three years old weighing three hundred pounds in a motorized wheelchair up in the Hollywood Hills, that Bobo killed. Wound a cord around his neck and didn't stop squeezing until the struggle was over. We'd gone up to have a talk with Doc 'cause he was giving us trouble in our transactions and him and Bobo got to quarreling, and Doc ordered us to leave—"Go home. Get out. I vanquish you. You are bad dreams—*I exorcise you!*"—shouting like he'd gone crazy. So Bobo quieted him.

Doc's grandniece Mignon was living there at the time, in a guest house that opened onto the pool. She might have heard the noise over the sound of her transistor but didn't investigate. Lifting barbells in the sun, in her swimsuit, hair the color of broom sage blowing wild in the wind. It was a dry scorching wind, late September. Fires up in the foothills and the smell of scorch in the air, not something's-going-to-happen but something already did.

Two, three years we'd been working with Doc through the private mail services then the old bastard says one day on the phone he can't fill our order, he's "retiring from the field," wants out, like it was that easy to break off with *us*. So we drove up. Uninvited but we drove up. "To what do I owe the honor of this visit?" Doc Junius asked in this snotty voice looking us over like we were dirt. *He* was some sort of a freak, so fat his skin looked as if it might not be able to hold him, beady turtle's eyes and fat loose wet lips and big hairy hard-breathing nostrils. Saying, "Nightmare apparitions come to life—acquiring visible form—but what, pray, have you to do with *me*?"

You could see the old guy was high—shot himself up every few hours with a secret concoction of his own. He rolled around in this fancy wheelchair with all the push-buttons, wheezing and snorting and chuckling to himself. What's so funny we asked him you old shit we tried to be reasonable but he laughed at us shaking his head like we really were some kind of ghosts not *there* in any way he had to respect, "—I banish you—vanish you—d'you hear? Out! Out! Away! At once!" His head was hairless as an eggshell, eyes weird-red, the floor gave way a little beneath him where he rolled. If Fritzie hadn't jumped aside Doc would have run over his foot. *Watch* it damn you Fritzie said but Doc wasn't watching or listening. Too far gone already!

Junius James Huizingo was Doc's full name. Wanted us to know he'd once been a renowned physician an internist by specialty then for no clear reason his patients abandoned him one by one, or died and failed to be replaced. The obituary in the *L.A. Times* would say he'd retired from the practice of medicine in 1967 after a malpractice suit of "scandalous dimensions."

Also that he was survived by only a grandniece, who shared his residence at the time of his death.

Our first meeting face to face old Doc tried to impress us with his hot-shit way of talking. Scrunched in his wheelchair eyeing us one by one like we were all sort of *equal*—the asshole way fancy talkers kid themselves that the language, *talk,* puts us all in the same boat. Saying in this slow wheezy voice like he thought somebody might want to write it down, "This world's a vale of tears but it can be overcome by *transcendence* and *scorn* in equal measure!"

Of the five of us it was Bobo listened hardest. What's *transcendence,* Doc, he asked. *Scorn* never gives me no trouble.

Doc's house was this Spanish-style hacienda place on a dead-end lane, fancy but wrecked-looking like it was abandoned. Weeds growing in the pink-gravel driveway and newspapers and other crap on the lawn that's all weeds too. Doc had a yard boy named Ramon he said but the little spic never showed up. Had a maid named Juanita but *she* never showed up. He had to feed himself which by the size of him he did O.K.—delivery things he could order by telephone, Chinese and Italian takeout. Before his niece came to live with him Doc said he'd been alone in the tunnel that's so long and so black—drawling *soooooo blaaaaack* and bugging out his eyes. If old fuckface wasn't so comical you'd naturally want to put him out of his misery was our common thought.

Still, said Doc, he was disappointed in Mignon over all. A girl so pretty—"She *is* pretty, boys, isn't she?—for so she strikes *me"*—yet so cold, icy-cold, so distant. It's heartrending said Doc. Perverse said Doc. Mignon accepted his hospitality scarcely thanking him as if it was her due. Actually she avoided him. Didn't share—let alone *prepare*—meals. Didn't converse with him except to say *Hello* sometimes, *How are you Uncle?* or *Nice day!*

A mysterious young woman Doc went on lowering his voice (though we could see Mignon plain as day out by the pool lifting barbells to the beat of her FM radio—she surely wasn't eavesdropping on *him*)—"Maybe you boys will have more luck making her acquaintance than I have had!" Bodybuilding was Mignon's life plus lying in the sun and sleeping ten, twelve hours a day and swimming in Doc's pool lazy and dreamy lap after lap after lap in the sparkling turquoise water not caring if anybody (for instance old wheezing pop-eyed Uncle) spied on her.

The five of us observed Mignon working out in her tiger-striped bikini. She wasn't ugly like a lot of female bodybuilders but she was solid muscle especially those hard tight perfect muscles in her shoulders and upper arms and her thighs, gleaming like copper. Actually a small woman about five foot three weighing maybe one hundred twenty pounds. Ash-blond hair and pale green eyes lifting out of the face never any smile or look of knowing who you are. That day one of us tried to talk to her saying *Meeg-non*—is that French? like that kind of a special cut of meat? and Mignon stared deadpan not answering like we didn't exist. Like there was just nothing there where we stood.

O.K. bitch we were thinking you're in line.

(Mignon drove a 1983 white Porsche. Old Doc Junius had a 1965 white Caddie never left the garage, the battery'd been dead for fifteen years. If we took Mignon away with us—some kind of a hostage, say—we'd have the Porsche too which was a good deal.)

Doc never invited us into his real house only the wing where he used to see patients. There was a sad stink of dirt and mice and old tobacco smoke, the tables in the waiting room were piled with *National Geographic, Reader's Digest, Boy's World, Life.* Those days, the five of us wore white: white polyester jackets, trousers, white T-shirts. Doc kept the place dark 'cause the sun gave him migraine he said so we were floating in the shadows grinning at one another like actual ghosts while old Doc babbled away calling us "my boys" and similar crap. He'd mix up Dago with Bobo, Fritzie with Brush, Brush with me, me with Dago which was an insult like he couldn't be troubled to learn our names.

In his inner office Doc kept a clear space around the desk where he could run his wheelchair 'round and 'round he said which aided in his thinking. At his age and in his condition Doc said you do a lot of thinking—that's about all you can do.

The day we had the trouble, Doc met us at the door and didn't want to let us in at first, talking loud and important like somebody on TV this shape like a three-hundred-pound sponge squeezed in a wheelchair. He was sweating globules of pearly lard and what we could see of his skin—his big bald head, his face, his hands—was dippled with liver spots like dirty water. Five months since we'd seen him and he looked older, puffed up under the skin, waterlogged. "Who are you? What claim do you have on me? What proof have you that *I* know *you*? *Why are you here?*" Excited and guilty not meeting our eyes saying, *"Why are you here?"*

So we looked at one another thinking the same thought. Like twins, the five of us.

When we drove up Mignon was swimming in the pool, and when the quarrel got serious she was working with her barbells and weights by the poolside so absorbed she didn't hear what was going on over the blast of her transistor or if she heard didn't care. Doc said he was *not* betraying us he was *not* working with someone else what he *was* was repenting of his ways before it was too late. Benzedrine, Dexedrine, Valium, Librium in such doses—some pharmacist was sure to get suspicious said Doc and we said O.K. Doc but why right now why right *now* and he hadn't any answer to that just repeating he wanted out, stammering and sputtering he was in terror of dying and wanted to repent his ways. Rolling in his wheelchair like a crazy son of a bitch you could feel the heat coming off of and his skin quivered and sagged like it was too thin to hold the fat inside. We looked through the stuff on top of his desk looked through the filing cabinet looking for prescription blanks and Doc said to keep our filthy hands off his things he'd call the police he'd trip the burglar alarm so loud and crazy there wasn't much else to do but what Bobo did: got behind him and wound a cord around his neck and choked and choked until it was over—which took some time.

All this while Mignon is doing her exercise routine not paying the slightest attention to us. We stuff all the blanks we can find in a valise and some syringes and other doctor's crap and search the house for cash and valuables of which there isn't much, smudging our finger-prints behind us, or trying to. Then we go out to where she is. Hey Mignon we say. Hey sweetheart guess what. Mignon's breathing a

little hard lifting a fifty-pound weight over her head her upper lip
damp with sweat and her skin gleaming with points of light like stars.
Hair still damp falling past her shoulder blades and those greeny-
green eyes cold as ice. Sweetheart we say clearing our throats nerved
up but sort of like teasing too we got some, y'know, serious talking
to do, your uncle and all, but Mignon continues with her workout
lifting and counting and not a one of us wants to interfere it's so
pleasurable to see, or more than pleasurable. Our five shadows on the
ground, watching.

So Mignon finishes the exercise and lays the weight down at her
feet with perfect poise. It's startling to see, her in her tiger bikini,
sweating and oily and every wisp of white-blond hair on her arms and
thighs standing out against the tan, *this is a lady.*

Looks at us for the first actual time, this calm scornful deadpan
kind of smile, says, "There's where you're wrong, fellas."

The Bystander

It happened so quickly, in such confusion, Mrs. Ingram would say afterward she hadn't had time to think, she'd done what she did without thinking. As if she thought it necessary to detach herself from the incident, not only from what had happened (which was ugly but not, these days, uncommon) but from the woman who had been involved in it, which was herself.

She was fifty-one years old. A woman of moderate height, not heavy, but compact; with firm shoulders, ample hips and thighs; rather foreshortened legs. Her thick black hair was threaded with gray and her eyebrows, thick too, and strikingly black, seemed to jut above her eyes, on a ridge of bone. As a young woman she'd been attractive, or rather handsome, with her slightly protuberant black eyes and mobile, fleshy mouth, but now her features looked exposed, drawn. Her skin was coarse and dry and of the hue of parchment and the flesh around her eyes had begun to crinkle as if in perplexity, or resentment. Her husband had left her when their children were still in high school, and had died before they were divorced; and she had never remarried. She had worked at a number of part-time jobs, clerking, waitressing, as an aide at the county hospital, she'd never owned property, only rented, and with the years her tendency to blame herself for wrongs committed against her—this was her daughter's opinion: her daughter, Sylvie, had many opinions—seemed to be increasing. She had never forgiven her husband for leaving her while at the same time she had not blamed him. ("It was a mistake, him marrying me. I guess he didn't know *me*.") If, at work, she believed herself slighted, or insulted, hurt pride required her to quit; but she never dared complain beforehand, let alone protest. ("I don't stick around where I'm not wanted," she told Sylvie. "I just move on.") She had graduated from an academically poor urban high school and had never, to her not quite secret shame, learned to read with much facility. It was her habit—and this too her children thought was increasing, as she aged—to go at things slantwise, and never head-on; to complain, for instance, of her landlord, or of her son's wife (who was "uncaring" of her), or of old friends, to anyone who would listen, but not to the offending parties themselves. (Sylvie said, "You're going to turn into an embittered old woman, Ma, is that what you want?" and Mrs. Ingram shrugged, and said, "What does it matter, what *I* want?—the world goes its own way. It always has.")

So Mrs. Ingram's behavior in the drugstore, that July evening, was the more puzzling; even, to her family, mysterious and disturbing, since there was no way by which, knowing her, they could satisfactorily explain it. She had gone into Cappy's, as the store was known in the neighborhood, just before closing, at about a quarter to nine; with the intention of making a few small purchases; and walked into what the police report would term a robbery in progress. She had not known what was going on, only that something strange was in the air, a tension, a stillness, in the very air, and even the light from the fluorescent tubing was wrong, everything too harsh and bright, and she'd heard, pushing into the store, a high-pitched voice that might have been a man's or a woman's, something on the radio maybe, even as she knew, or seemed to know, it wasn't the radio; the store was otherwise quiet; and looked empty. She knew that something was wrong but made no move to turn around and leave though at that point—the gunman hadn't seen her—it would have been possible to leave. It was as if momentum of a kind pushed her along, like a wave, or waves, dreamily pushing her along, and in, and toward, what was happening at the rear of the store; like water swirling down a drain. She would say afterward, I guess I just couldn't stop.

The clerk at Cappy's was the college-age son of a friend of Mrs. Ingram's, one of her oldest friends, with whom she'd gone to school decades before, and this woman, Annalee Knoth, was a widow too, and had had, the previous winter, an operation to remove a cancerous growth from her colon, so there was that connection, if a tenuous one; a not quite articulated sense of maternal responsibility and obligation. But she'd probably have done the same thing, Mrs. Ingram said, if she hadn't known the boy at the cashier's counter, if he'd been as much a stranger to her as the gunman himself whom she'd never seen before in the neighborhood yet who looked to her, she couldn't have said why, familiar somehow, a scruffy youngish man, in his early thirties, wearing a sweaty tank top and low-riding jeans and his hair frizzed from the heat, a tiny gold-glinting stud in one of his earlobes, a tattoo of some kind, though it appeared faded, or smeared, on his left bicep, and these wild quick-darting frightened eyes that took her in as she approached—high on some drug, Mrs. Ingram thought, knowing of such things, of "crack" in particular, by way of the daily paper and the evening television news. Afterward it would be revealed that the gunman had a record of numerous prior arrests and a conviction, for armed robbery, assault, and possession of a deadly weapon, he'd served four years of a twelve-year sentence at one of the state prisons, and these facts, or their equivalents, Mrs. Ingram had also known, as she'd sensed—this would be part of her account, given to police—that he meant to kill the Knoth boy after robbing him. He had that look, Mrs. Ingram said—his eyes, his crazy eyes, a killer who had to be stopped.

The gunman was behind the cashier's counter and Jerry Knoth was just getting down, on his hands and knees, to lie on the floor, on his stomach, as the gunman had ordered him to do, and Mrs. Ingram called out loudly, "What are you doing? What is this?"—or something similar; she wouldn't remember, afterward, her exact words; only that they were quick, and loud, pushy angry words of a kind she'd never heard herself say before, in any public place. It was like she'd gone back decades to when the children were young, and the way you spoke to them half the time was scolding, disciplining, since half the time they were getting into trouble and that was the only way they could be made to listen, to take what you said seriously.

The gunman said something to Mrs. Ingram she couldn't hear, and she saw the gun in his hand, trembling in his hand, it was like a dream in which everything is stopped so you can see it clearly but you can't react, can't get away, and still she came forward, she was saying, loudly, "Don't! Don't you do it!"—knowing he was about to shoot, and there was nothing she could do except to unnerve him, to make him miss. His first shot struck some bottles on a shelf maybe eight inches from her head, and now she was stopped, still, paralyzed, and a memory came to her of other times in her life she'd gone too far, made a mistake, like walking through mud she hadn't supposed was quite so deep, and there was a point it was easier to go forward than back, though not easy in any case. So she screamed, "Get out of here! Get out of here! Leave him alone! The police are right outside!"—words that simply came to her out of nowhere, out of an expediency she must have absorbed not so much from years of having watched television crime programs—in fact she rarely watched them—as of having lived in a culture that watched them, in which any citizen might, under sufficient duress, pull stray lines of dialogue out of the very air. The gunman was staring at Mrs. Ingram as if she was crazy, and he couldn't deal with a crazy woman, and he might simply have fled, taking no money, shooting no one, if she hadn't been in his way. His second shot caught her in the left shoulder, ripping through the flesh, shattering the bone, with a power that literally threw her backward; and there was a sound of breaking glass, and Mrs. Ingram's screams, and she was on the floor, dazed, dripping blood, seeing the floor a few inches from her face, a filthy floor splattered with blood. The shock of the wound was so great she didn't feel any pain, or much pain; only a sense, still, of doing the right thing, of asserting herself and her power; of triumphing over the gunman; and of having no choice in the matter.

The gunman pushed past her and escaped. There was a sound of

someone whimpering close by. "Jerry?" Mrs. Ingram said. "Did he
hurt you?" She tried to get to her feet but fell again, heavily, and when
she woke, an unfathomable period of time later, she was in the
emergency room of St. Luke's Hospital, being treated, as the young
doctor told her, for a gunshot wound. And she saw that everything
would fall into place: the pain in her shoulder (she now felt pain, and
it was considerable) was from a bullet; she'd been shot in an attempted robbery, at Cappy's; she'd been shot as the gunman fled, and
he'd fled without injuring the young clerk, Jerry Knoth, and without
taking any money from the cash register. So this is how it is, she
thought. She would have smiled, except for the pain, and being so
publicly exposed; the doctor and the nurses standing over her. So this
is how it is turning out.

Later, she and the Knoth boy described the would-be robber to the
police. She'd seen him, evidently, far more clearly than Jerry had;
she'd made it a point, she said, to memorize his appearance. Aged
thirty-one or -two, weight about one hundred fifty, the heat-frizzed
hair, the coarse-pored swarthy skin, the bluish cast of his two-day
beard; the gold stud in his left earlobe and the tattoo on his left bicep;
the tank-top shirt and the bleached, soiled blue jeans. Amid a hundred photographs Mrs. Ingram quickly found his photograph: There.
That's the one. And Jerry Knoth agreed, after a moment's hesitation.
He hadn't really seen the man's face in much detail, he confessed.
He'd been too damned scared.

The people at the hospital, and the police detectives, and, later, her
family and friends, all said of Mrs. Ingram that she'd acted bravely.
She had prevented the robbery at Cappy's, for whatever that was
worth. Because he was an excitable boy, a sweet good-natured im-
pressionistic boy, Jerry Knoth went about saying that she'd saved his
life; which might, or might not, have been true. Mrs. Ingram believed
she'd done nothing for which she might claim credit, since she had
acted without thinking; she'd acted first, and thought about it afterward. Which wasn't like her, really. If you knew her.

The one thing she remembered from the incident, which she liked
remembering, though it would have been difficult to explain to another person, was that she'd done what had to be done; she'd set her
strength, her power, her willfulness, against that of the gunman
(whose name, she learned, was Perez, Julio Perez: though she didn't
much like his having a name), and she had won. He'd shot her
through the shoulder, and her shoulder would never be the same
again for the rest of her life, and she'd wake out of nightmares of
gunfire and breaking glass for the rest of her life, but she'd set herself
against him and she'd won; and she knew it, and he knew it; would
have to acknowledge it, even if, when they were again in each other's
presence, at various hearings at the county courthouse, and, eventually, at the brief juryless trial in November, the man never looked at
her. He disdained to look at her, or he was fearful of looking at her,
a middle-aged woman, a woman old enough to be his mother, at
whom he'd shot point-blank, meaning to kill; but had failed to kill.
Mrs. Ingram was required each time to identify the gunman by
pointing at him, and so she did, saying quietly, "Yes. That's the
man," but still he did not look at her. Her heart knocked against her
ribs, in angry elation. She had won, she had triumphed. That fact
could never be altered.

While her shoulder was healing, to the degree it would heal, and she
was still in the hospital, at St. Luke's, Mrs. Ingram's daughter, Sylvie,
visited her every day, and her son dropped by after work. They were
adult versions of their adolescent selves, inclined, when they were
alone with their mother, to show their unmediated feelings; in this
case bewilderment, hurt, even resentment. What had made her do it?
standing up to a man with a gun? a robber, a criminal? for all she
knew, a killer? Sylvie and Carl stared at their mother as if they'd
never seen her before; they couldn't grasp the logic, even the illogic,
of what she'd done. "It was just something that happened," Mrs.
Ingram said evasively. "I didn't think about it, like I told the police
I didn't have time to think about it, why don't we change the sub-

ject?" Still they persisted, as if her behavior had something to do with
them, reflected in some public way upon them; constituted a kind of
betrayal. Sylvie was the more adamant, Sylvie couldn't seem to let it
rest. Sitting at her mother's bedside frowning and asking was it
because of Jerry Knoth? she'd been scared the gunman would shoot
him? "You could have let him take care of himself, Ma, you know,"
Sylvie said, "—a kid that age. What is he, twenty-five?" "He's
twenty-one." "Yes but still. Old enough to take care of himself."
Sylvie paused; she was a handsome big-boned girl, with her mother's
eyes and facial bones, a shy stubbornness in her manner. "You weren't thinking of your own family, that's for damned sure."

I wasn't thinking of anything, Mrs. Ingram thought. So damn you
let me alone.

A reporter from the local newspaper came, and interviewed Mrs.
Ingram, and there appeared in the following Sunday's paper an arti-
cle headlined "BYSTANDER THWARTS HOLD-UP ATTEMPT," accompanied by a photograph of "Mrs. Gladys Ingram of Schiller Avenue"
trussed up in her hospital bed, unsmiling, eyes narrowed against the
camera's flash, but looking peaceful enough, even happy, get-well
cards and pots of flowers on the table beside her bed. Following the
newspaper piece she received more cards, some flowers, some letters,
from both acquaintances in the city and total strangers. "Too much
fuss," she laughed, though of course she was secretly pleased. There
was no particular merit in having acted bravely, if indeed she had
acted bravely; except it singled her out as she'd always dreaded, and
hoped, she might be singled out. For hadn't she known since girlhood
that she was . . . in some way special . . . though the way in which
she was special had never defined itself to her.

For months after the shooting people told her she was lucky,
damned lucky, to be alive, and Mrs. Ingram always said, pressing her
hand against her heart as if in confirmation that her heart was still
beating, "Yes. I am. Lucky to be alive." And she felt her luck like
sunshine flooding her body, warming it, enlivening it, and the near-
perpetual ache in her shoulder did not seem to her too great a price

to pay, for that warmth. In November Julio Perez pleaded guilty to
felonious assault, armed robbery, and a weapon charge, and was
sentenced to fifteen years in prison, this time fifteen years minimum,
so he'd be out of the way for a long, long time, that must be a relief
to you everyone said but in truth Mrs. Ingram would not have
worried about Perez anyway; he was but the instrument, the vehicle,
of her specialness, and did not figure, much, in her fantasies about
herself, or about the future.

Now she knew the craziness in her she lay awake long nights thinking
of what she'd do next, a new apartment or duplex to which she might
move, giving her landlord the latest possible notice, new furniture
she'd buy, and why not a trip to Tampa this winter, her cousin Agnes
was always inviting her down (and she'd never flown on an airplane,
at her age: what was she waiting for?). There was a man she knew
from church, his wife had died only a few years before, and he
managed a hardware store downtown, he looked at Gladys Ingram
sometimes in a certain way, sweet-smiling and a little hurt, a way she
understood, and why not him, for Christ's sake why not, she lay
awake smiling into the dark stretching and yawning plotting all the
things she'd do, the two of them moving away together maybe to
Florida, for why not, what was keeping her here after all. She would
show Carl and Carl's stuck-up wife, she would show Sylvie whom
she'd never quite forgiven, for the girl's mean spirit at the time Mr.
Ingram had moved out . . . blaming *her* for the failure of the marriage
how dare anyone blame *her* . . . after all she'd suffered. And lottery
tickets: she'd go wild and buy a half-dozen next time: why the hell
not? She'd have her hair cut and styled, a black rinse to get rid of the
gray, she'd lose a few pounds, buy some new clothes, fifty-one wasn't
really old though she'd been acting old, feeling old, for years. Oh she
was going to start! She'd get herself going! Soon, very soon!

    In the end nothing came of it. But that was what Mrs. Ingram
plotted, those nights.

Shelter

In the capital city of the northernmost country of their itinerary Cecilia Heath and Philip Schoen are taken by their embassy guide to visit an underground bomb shelter behind Parliament Square. "It's a remarkable feat of architectural design," the guide says, "—something you don't want to miss." The guide's name is Keith. His manner is direct, rather boyish. Of course he is an American like Cecilia and Philip but he has lived abroad so long—nearly fifteen years—that his accent has become flat, neutral, indefinable. He can speak an impressive variety of languages—Arabic, Japanese, Greek, Swedish, even some Finnish. He went into the foreign service, he says, at the age of twenty-five, and has never once regretted it.

Late one afternoon he drives them in an embassy car along the narrow cobblestoned streets behind the Parliament buildings. There are few pedestrians on the sidewalks in this part of the city, no cars parked at the curbs. The street names are all incomprehensible—the language of this country is a truly foreign language. Cecilia notes that the street on which they park is dim and featureless, mainly walls, brick, concrete blocks, a few aluminum garage doors. Keith explains that the bomb shelter is a state secret. Yet of course it isn't, since so many civilians know about it, or believe they know about it. "However," Keith says, "they don't talk about it."

He takes them to one of the large aluminum doors in which, oddly, there is a smaller door of nearly normal proportions. The aluminum is battered and oil-stained, the pavement underfoot is cracked. From out of a vest pocket he draws a key of ordinary dimensions, a house key, perhaps, and fits it into the lock. Philip asks if very many people have keys to the shelter and Keith says politely, "No, naturally not." Philip then asks who has access to it and Keith says, distracted, as he turns the key in one direction and then in the other, "Well— Members of Parliament and high government officials, of course. A number of favored diplomats. And distinguished visitors to the country if there happen to be any at the time of attack."

"What about the others?" Cecilia asks. "The millions of others—?"

The lock is codified and it is necessary for Keith to get it exactly right. In a vague cheery voice he says, "You might want to take a deep breath of this fresh air because the air inside isn't . . . isn't so fresh."

At last the lock clicks, the door is opened.

As they step inside Keith says, in reply to Cecilia's question, "Of course there are other bomb shelters, more conventional shelters, built during the war."

He switches on a panel of fluorescent lights. What they can see of the interior is concrete walls, a flight of steps, a landing, and more steps, leading out of sight. The air is fiercely cold and stagnant, smelling of damp, earth, dust, rodent droppings. Cecilia's instinct, which she controls, is to gag; Philip's is to laugh as if something were amusing. "It *is* a formidable place, isn't it," Keith says, allowing the heavy door to swing shut behind them and lock.

He leads them down the first flight of steps, walking cautiously. The steps are unusually steep. "Sometimes people have odd reactions down here," he says conversationally, "but of course there's nothing to be apprehensive about. It's perfectly empty and it's perfectly safe. In fact I find it rather comforting."

Cecilia tries to think of the place as a kind of cellar, a cold storage vault. Certainly there isn't any danger. Certainly they can't be trapped down here. The guide's voice, somewhat high-pitched, is echoing from the ceiling; his brisk footsteps ring. Something is vibrat-

ing finely—it must be the railing. As they descend the air gets colder
and ranker. On the first landing there is an enormous poster on the
wall giving instructions, presumably, in that indecipherable language.
Keith reads out parts of it—emergency drill, precautions to take,
stations to report to. On the second landing there is a six-foot dummy
in full nuclear defense regalia: khaki-colored jacket and trousers,
boots, gas mask, gloves.

"This is your basic issue," Keith says, indicating the dummy's
costume. "It looks more oppressive than it really is—in fact it's fairly
lightweight."

Cecilia stares at the dummy, waiting for it to move, to speak.
Perhaps because it is so shrewdly prepared for disaster—perhaps
because of the gas mask—she attributes to it powers of a sort she
knows she doesn't herself possess. As a child, shopping with her
mother in clothing stores, she often felt the mannequins watching her
closely.

Downward, ever downward Keith guides them, giving a brief history of the shelter, speaking of the prime minister (former, defeated)
who opposed the construction of the shelter and of the prime minister
(current, with a respectable backing in Parliament) who supported it.
He shows them the pitch-black passageway that leads secretly into
the shelter from the Parliament buildings, and the equally pitch-black
passageway that leads from the prime minister's residence. There is
a storeroom for provisions of all sorts, including food, gallons of
mineral water, and medical supplies—an enormous space, the size of
a small warehouse; there is an infirmary; there is an emergency
assembly room. The shelter is computer-controlled, or will be, in time
of attack. Note the television monitors, the telephones. And along
this corridor (he switches on the wavering fluorescent lights) are
rooms equipped with cots, bunkbeds, sinks, lavatories. . . . "Some of
the more luxurious rooms are even equipped with showers," Keith
says. He opens one of the doors, with difficulty, and invites them to
peer inside.

Cecilia leans inside and smells something rancid, vaguely feculent,

as if a toilet had backed up; she has to resist the impulse once again
to gag. The cell-like room awaits its occupant, flat mattress and
pillow laid upon a spring-cot, bedclothes folded neatly at the foot.
Philip turns on the light switch but the light fails to respond.

"It isn't bad, is it," says Keith. "Especially when you consider the
alternative."

"What is the alternative?" Cecilia asks calmly.

Keith exchanges a glance with Philip, clearly meant for Cecilia to
see. "Are you a disarmament person?" he asks her with a courteous
smile.

"Are you a war person?" asks Cecilia.

Keith laughs as if she had said something witty. Over the last few
minutes his voice has grown steadily more assured, more at ease, but
Cecilia still cannot determine any accent. He might be from Texas,
or Maryland, or Oregon, or Maine. In the subtly flickering fluorescent light his eyes are the color of washed glass and his skin has been
bleached gray. He looks like an ancient child. "I don't like to be
reduced to a political stance, Miss Heath, any more than you do,"
he says evenly. "Of course the shelter is a sobering place—it isn't
meant to be cheering, like a luxury hotel—but the fact that it *is*, it
exists, is something we have to contend with."

"How long could anyone survive down here?" Cecilia asks. "I
mean as human beings, sane human beings—? Think of the terror,
the disorientation, the hopelessness—"

"But the alternative is absolute terror," Keith says, "—and disorientation—and hopelessness. One is a gamble of sorts but the other
is a certainty."

"The other *isn't* a certainty."

"Given the terms of the predicament—"

Philip interrupts, drawing Keith aside. He wants to ask him a few
questions, he says, and Keith is grateful for the diversion. When was
the shelter commissioned?—how long did it take to build?—who
designed it?—is it similar, or even identical, to other bomb shelters
in Western Europe or in the States? Cecilia carefully closes the door

of the cell and follows along behind the men, in no hurry to catch up. All her senses are sharpened, on edge. She is thinking of the heavy door that swung closed upon them up on the street level—like the door to a meat locker. She is thinking of the cold air, the fresh air, the queer pitiless blue of the northern sky. Her nostrils contract against the faint stench of dirt, damp, earth, rot. Certainly she smells rot. Something has died down here, the air is poisoned, the three of them, three idiots, are being gradually poisoned as they stroll about taking in the sights, gaping at costumed dummies, lightless rooms. *We're surrounded by earth,* she thinks. *This is really a tomb and we are buried alive.*

Philip and Keith are deeply involved in their conversation. Philip's manner is direct, curious, slightly amused—for his general style is to mask emotion of any kind behind an air of detached amusement. How many levels are there to the shelter?—how many square yards of space?—how many entrances, exits?—what sort of computer controls it?—how much did it cost to build, how much to maintain?—do the M.P.'s and the others go through regular emergency drills?—how many missiles (as of, say, last week) are aimed at the city from Soviet Russia? How much of a warning do they expect in case of attack?

Keith smiles an odd wavering smile and draws one hand rapidly through his hair. "Do you mean—how much warning will we have if we're lucky, or if we aren't—?" he says.

It is twelve exhausting days since Cecilia and Philip flew out, at seven in the evening, from Kennedy Airport; and ten days until they are scheduled to return from Frankfurt. So the visit to the bomb shelter falls strategically at midpoint.

At a protracted luncheon in the ambassador's residence that day they were talking of the self-conscious neutrality, the pained caution, of this nation. Facing West while facing East, to coin a phrase. A diplomacy of exquisite and often ingenious tact. A diplomacy of shrewdness or of cowardice, depending upon one's prejudices.

"They know they can't afford to offend us," said the ambassador, "but they certainly can't afford to offend the Russians either. Their political humor seems to turn upon Soviet paranoia, at least what we hear. For instance, a native and a visitor are strolling along the seawall, and the native says, 'The ocean freezes here in mid-winter, all the way to Russia,' and the visitor says, 'To make it easier for the tanks to drive across?' " He paused, making a playful face. "Then there is the frequent expression, which you might find puzzling when you first hear it—it's invariably delivered in a flat droll voice with a shake of the head: 'The light doesn't always shine from the East.' "

" 'The light doesn't always shine from the—?' Oh yes I see," Cecilia said.

The ambassador acknowledged that such humor was fairly innocuous by American standards. "They don't expect us to laugh," he said. "A sympathetic smile, maybe . . ."

The visit to the bomb shelter is to require no more than a half-hour of their time—a small portion, after all, of their visit to Europe.

And the shelter is in its primary sense a physical structure; an architectural experiment; an underground dormitory of sorts, hooked up with sophisticated machines. There are a number of ways of interpreting it quite apart from the narrowly political.

Cecilia thinks of an Egyptian pyramid, a city of the dead. The elaborate monument to death. In this case the pyramid is reversed, descending into the earth, burrowing downward to eternal life.

"Not a city of the dead," her guide corrects her, startled, smiling, "—a city of the *living*. A city of *survivors.*"

Come see what's in the ditch here, the boys called to Cecilia, many years ago, almost thirty years ago—c'mere, *c'mere!*—their voices lifting innocently, slyly.

Cecilia thrust her knuckles into her mouth and ran past without looking. Yet she must have looked—in one terrible helpless instant she must have looked—because for months and years afterward when she shut her eyes tight in bed, in the dark, or stared at a featureless wall, she saw again the mangled corpse with the matted fur, she saw the sickening swirling motion, the white, the maggots in the raccoon's (or was it a groundhog's) bloodied snout.

What is mankind's secret, most shameful whisper?—burrowing head downward in the dark, clutching hard, gathering strength, heat. *I don't want to die. Please don't let me die. If others die will I live forever . . . ?*

Cecilia is sickened by the bomb shelter and tells herself that she is angry, no she is frightened, no in fact she is overcome by a sensation of boredom. How many more minutes? Surely it is time to leave, to brave those interminable steps?

Cecilia is not jealous of Philip and Keith's remarkable rapport. She does not care to hear what they are saying. She notes how, in the uncertain light, their faces are identically bleached and their shadows have dissolved. (Yet something resembling a shadow—vaporous, ghostly—floats lightly at their feet.)

Cecilia does not mind being left behind. In fact she dawdles, walks slower, stops to inspect one of the posters as if seeking out a single word she might recognize. (But there is none. This language, as she has known all along, is distinctly foreign, with no relationship to English at all.)

Idly, ignoring the fact that her fingers are shaking, she pauses to examine one of the dummies. He is tall, wide-shouldered, athletic in build, confident. The khaki jacket and trousers fit him quite well, the gloves are perhaps less convincing. Cecilia lifts the gas mask to see a blank blue-eyed face, neutral of expression, with pursed lips and a febrile ruddy skin.

Suddenly the dummy's predicament, his imminent death, strikes her as both painful and embarrassing.

Cecilia Heath owes this arduous trip abroad to Philip Schoen's inter-
vention in her behalf at the Foundation. He is interviewing prospec-
tive fellows for three-year residencies in the States and he asked the
director of the Foundation if Cecilia might accompany him. The trip
would, he told Cecilia, give them a chance to become acquainted with
each other. Yes, said Cecilia, how could it *not*—? She thought herself
naively shrewd in checking out the fact that Heath and Schoen were
booked for two separate hotel rooms throughout the tour.

Philip Schoen happens to be married and the father of two
nearly grown children, whom Cecilia hopes never to meet. His
marriage, as he tells her, has shifted to another tense—past, past
perfect. Hence his chronic amused melancholy, his embarrassed
cynicism. ("A middle-aged husband's dissatisfaction with his wife
is his dissatisfaction with himself," Philip has told Cecilia wittily,
"—but how am I to divorce myself?") Cecilia is the sort of woman
who examines her mirrored reflection primarily as an act of pen-
ance; Philip's interest arouses both her gratitude and her unease.

(At the Foundation it has been said of her, in jest, affectionately,
more or less behind her back, that Cecilia Heath has forgotten she
is female, if indeed anyone ever told her; she's famously absorbed in
her work, abstracted and remote. But in fact Cecilia knows very well
that she is female—it's her womanliness that troubles her.)

Cecilia is tall, willowy, soft-spoken, physically shy, with odd angu-
lar features that sometimes appear handsome and at other times
remain merely odd. Her chestnut-red hair is haphazardly streaked
with gray, the taut skin over her cheekbones is flushed as if permanently sunburnt, her eyes are a muted somber green, clouded with
thought. She imagines herself a looming presence, awkward and
unsettling; it can't be an accident that her expensive clothes are
usually a size or two too large. She would like to inhabit her body
as she inhabits her clothes—with an air of mildly ironic detachment.
"An old maid," she thinks, catching sight of her reflection when she
isn't prepared for it, "—a Crazy Jane," she thinks, wondering at the
streaked red hair that always looks windblown, the prim ill-fitting

clothes, the fleshy mouth with its air of baffled discontent. Like many solitary people Cecilia has the habit of talking with herself but her conversations never come to anything.

She doesn't know if her growing sense of agitation on this three-week tour is a consequence of her feeling for Philip Schoen, or the consequence of visiting too many countries in too brief a period of time. Travel disorients her, makes her heart and pulse race, wears her soul dangerously thin. Philip has said that the world is divided into travelers and tourists, that travelers are admirable, tourists contemptible; but Cecilia knows which she is. And she does lack ambition.

Suddenly, without warning, the fluorescent lights emit a harsh crackling noise—and go out.

And the shelter is plunged into darkness.

Someone exclaims, startled, chagrined—it must be the guide.

Cecilia feels perspiration break out everywhere on the surface of her body, despite the cold. But she speaks in an oddly normal voice, telling Keith where she is, explaining that she'll grope her way toward them. (The men are standing approximately twenty, twenty-five feet away, near the base of the steps: they had been about to leave the shelter.)

Philip calls out her name in a falsely hearty and comforting way, as if she required immediate solicitude; Keith says loudly that everything is all right—there's no danger—a switch must have been thrown, or the power simply failed—temporarily. *There is no danger and no one should panic.*

Cecilia gropes her way forward, stumbling like a drunk. She has the wild idea that the ventilation system has already gone off and that they will be poisoned within a few minutes. Her teeth are chattering, her heart trips lightly and crazily, but her voice, when she speaks, is resolutely calm. In a way this blackout doesn't surprise her—she must have been expecting some sort of mishap all along.

After a minute's confusion Cecilia and Philip, arms outstretched, blunder together and grasp hands: now they are partway safe. Keith insists that they can't possibly be in danger, it's a simple power failure, they will have no trouble climbing the steps in the dark. "The important thing of course is not to panic," he says. But his voice has gone shrill and breathless.

In all, it seems to take a very long time for the three of them to grope their way up the stairs. Keith pushes ahead as if he were leading a rescue mission, the sort of thing for which he has been trained as a member of the American diplomatic corps. He calls down useless instructions, repeating there's no danger, can't possibly be any danger, they can't possibly be trapped, it's a simple power failure. "Are you both all right?" he asks urgently. "Are you following me? Miss Heath—? Mr. Schoen—? No cause for alarm—"

Cecilia and Philip, taking the steps doggedly, one at a time, fall into a fit of bizarre laughter, like guilty children. It must be Keith they are laughing at though they don't mean to be cruel.

("*Are* you all right?" Philip asks Cecilia. "Your fingers are like ice." Cecilia says, "*Your* fingers are like ice.")

The steps appear to be steeper than before. But finite, surely. It is all a matter of climbing them slowly, hanging onto the railing, not giving in to dark turbulent counterproductive thought. Cecilia's breath is audible, a vein beats in her throat. She might be terrified or in a state of intense rage. She might be confirmed in her suspicion that they have all died, the incident is merely history (and anecdotal history at that—scarcely to be taken seriously).

I don't want to die, a tiny voice murmurs, —*must I die?*

But of course the three of them navigate the steps perfectly. They are adults, responsible adults, the situation after all isn't—as Keith keeps insisting—a really serious one. They aren't in danger of suffocating. The world isn't erupting above them in a holocaust of flame and tempestuous winds. When the door is finally unlocked—when they step out onto the sidewalk—the air will be cold and clear and fresh, just as they remember.

If others die, will I be spared? —But Cecilia has no time to attend to this small mad voice. She and Philip stand waiting in the dark as, groping, panting, their guide tries to fit his key into the invisible lock.

Party

Judith Lambert was dying at last. She had come home from the Medical Center for the fifth and final time in how many months?—eighteen?—since her cancer was first diagnosed. But the Institute party was scheduled for that night, the handwritten invitations sent out weeks ago, so they were at the party, Judith's many friends and a number of her colleagues from the Bedminister Choir College, where Judith had taught voice for fifteen years, how sad they were saying, how tragic, she is such a young woman, —forty-seven: and looks ten years younger despite the chemotherapy—gathered about the long candlelit table where plates of hors d'oeuvres were set amidst coolly fragrant spring flowers, daffodils, jonquils, hyacinth, taking up Swedish meatballs on toothpicks, jumbo shrimp dipped in Mexicali hot sauce (Take care, the director's wife warns, —that sauce *is* hot), how lovely everything looks tonight, and this wine, this is superb wine, German, is it? and how delicious the stuffed mushrooms, did you make these yourself, Isabel? Judith Lambert's spring concert last year was a great success everyone said, I wasn't able to get to it myself because I had to be out of town, yes you missed a lovely concert Judith sang songs by Schumann, Schubert, Fauré, I think, miniatures, most of them, such a fine clear beautiful voice she had, something plaintive about it, not strong of course, not powerful, once I

heard her sing that Mozart aria *"Bella mia fiamma"* and you could
tell she'd reached her limit but she had a haunting voice, it's all such
a pity. Judith's daughter was saying, Mother?—please, Mother?—are
you awake, Mother? The bedroom was papered in a floral design,
fine-patterned, French silk, lavender, soft green, ivory, matching bedspread and a thick ivory carpet, Ginny Mullins had visited her the
week before, It's so sad she said, tears welling in her eyes, yes she has
changed a good deal now, she looks so frail, so thin, thank God her
daughter is with her, and thank God for morphine. A new couple had
just entered the hall, shaking hands with the Institute director Dr.
Max and his wife, Isabel, tall flaxen-haired sharp-eyed Isabel, if you
decline one of her invitations she will never invite you back. That
dinner party Judith gave at Christmas, —there must have been
twenty of us and she tried to do it all herself, not even a student to
help in the kitchen, of course it was a buffet, and not so much trouble:
but still. And do you know I never got around to inviting her back,
this season has been sheer madness, we were in Minneapolis, and we
were in Atlanta, and where else, Los Angeles of course. I am reminded of a line from a play, or is it a poem, *Shall I ever have time
to die?* the heroine asks. Her doctor said she'd have a year to live with
the treatments, I think that was terribly blunt, and cruel, don't you,—
and wrong by about six months too. She has been taking chemotherapy off and on all this time and the wonder of it is, her hair, her lovely
hair, didn't fall out: can you imagine Judith without her lovely red
hair? So brave, such a model of courage, endurance, such a vital
attitude toward the future,—this cheese is exquisite, is it some kind
of Italian cheese—*this* is goat cheese, Mark you must try it—her
attitude was so positive it was daunting sometimes, the way she spoke
of the future, plans for next year's concert series at Bedminister, and
the year *after,* Mark says it was a necessary blindness, a kind of
denial, where did you get this pâté, Isabel?—it's duck isn't it? —That
little store on Charity Street, off South Street, do you know the one
I mean? Yes I've seen it but I haven't gone inside. I feel so bad about
Judith, that lovely party she gave and I never invited her back, it's

so awkward with a single woman at a sit-down dinner don't you think. Did I tell you, Mark is flying to Johannesburg on Monday, some sort of confidential government business, I'm concerned there will be a civil war while he's there and he won't be able to get out. Judith looked so lovely at the Christmas concert, directing the women's choir, that white dress she wore that looked like an antique dress,—full-skirted, flounced, with ruffles at her throat, long sleeves, lacy cuffs—I think it was to disguise the fact she'd lost so much weight. Oh just the *Messiah* I think—the usual. Yes it was a shame about Rod leaving her but it seems to have worked out for the best, Judith was the happiest I've ever seen her after the divorce came through, there's no bitterness between them that anyone ever noticed, though there must have been some emotion involved, you can't be married for twenty years without some emotion being involved, yes but the daughter is grown up, all our children are grown up. Have you noticed, it has happened so quickly: all our children are grown up, and most of them are moved away. A faint sickle moon was shining through the tall leaded windows of the Institute's main hall, where one hundred guests were gathered, and a string quartet played in a corner, on a raised platform edged with flowers. In the din of voices no one could hear the music but the musicians, good sports from the Bedminister school, played briskly on: something by Beethoven, it sounded like. Is that the moon? Where? In the trees. There. The moon?—I don't think so, it looks like one of the lights in the parking lot. Mother, said Judith's daughter, —can you hear me? Are you awake? Mother I love you, Judith's daughter said, but it wasn't clear that Judith heard. The skin around her eyes looked stitched, bruised pouches beneath the eyes, it must be the mask of death since Judith is dying but her daughter stands transfixed unable to judge. I remember Roslyn Lambert when she was a little girl passing plates of hors d'oeuvres at one of their parties, a lawn party it was, Rod and Judith certainly gave the impression of being happily married then, such an attractive couple, Judith looked like one of those Pre-Raphaelite women, you know the ones I mean, didn't that artist

who lived in the Hawleys' coach house paint her?—and what came
of the portrait, I wonder? His new wife is very sweet they say though
I've never met her, one of his graduate students evidently. Doesn't
time pass swiftly now! And incessantly! They were talking of the new
women's choir director, the blond young woman from Juilliard
whose husband is assistant dean at the seminary. An attractive young
couple but there are so many attractive young couples these days.
Thank you so *much* Isabel for inviting us. Thank *you* for coming but
isn't it a little early to be leaving? I called Judith last week but Roslyn
said she was sleeping and couldn't be disturbed, she spoke rather
sharply to me, I thought, I *was* a bit hurt, after all I've been a friend
of Judith's for so long and was one of the first people Judith told. Max
said he'd bought a case of this by way of that dealer in Pennsfield,
Bernkasteler Doktor Auslese 1982, not what you'd call cheap but it
was a bargain. The funeral will be next week probably, and the
memorial service has to be planned, not until May I suppose. Did you
go to Dr. Emory's memorial?—it was fairly well attended but I was
surprised at the people missing you'd have expected to see there. He
was so well loved, his students adored him. That's usually the case,
this time of year. It's madness this time of year. I'm committed to a
conference in Geneva next week I wish I could get out of, a week-long
session in Tokyo next month, loans and financing for the Third
World, more of the same thing, the situation is hopeless and getting
worse but don't quote me. Is Judith's daughter with her? No? I
thought someone said she was. She *is?* I heard they'd hired a private
nurse, I guess you have to, in cases like this, dying at home, poor
Judith, but at least she's in comfortable surroundings, and where is
Rod? —He won't dare miss the funeral but he hasn't visited her in
a year. He's very big, they say, at La Jolla: found his niche at last.
Did Florence tell you, they're having a reception for the French
ambassador next week, I hope there isn't going to be an awkward
conflict with the funeral. Judith closed her skeletal fingers around her
daughter's wrist and seemed about to smile as she so frequently did
though her eyes flashed with panic but this time she did not smile,

she whispered, Help me, and her daughter said, I'm right here, Mother, I'm not going to go away. A faint moon through the window, in the trees beyond the house, hazy like the lamplight in the room, the only light burning, filtered through the fluted flesh-colored shade. Our new astrophysicist is being wooed by the California Institute of Technology already, did you hear?—it's outrageous. Everyone bids on the stars and no one much wants the others. I hope I won't be out of town for the party, this time of year is such madness. Are those dogwood sprays? Apple blossom? *So* lovely. Shall I ever have time to die, she wondered. She was staring into a corner of the room where friends with the look of strangers were talking and laughing loudly. Someday yes. Judith's daughter dialed the number she knew by heart and said into the receiver, calm as words said many times, I think she has died. Yes. A few minutes ago. The funeral will be this week, the memorial service in early May, we'll have to get together with those boring Bedminister people to plan it. At the door Ginny Mullins squeezed my hand and whispered in my ear, The invitations should be in the mail by next Friday but remember: keep the night of May 11 open. For us.

Stroke

Her father was not an old man but he'd had a sudden stroke and it was serious they said so she terminated her lecture tour—she had "done" West Germany and Belgium and had only Holland, that is, Amsterdam, ahead—and flew home on the earliest available flight, arriving at John F. Kennedy Airport at what was presumably the late afternoon while simultaneously the late morning of the very day she'd started in, thinking God don't let him die, don't let him die God though not in the nuances of prayer, you cannot after all have an angry prayer nor had she believed in God for a very long time. She rented a car and drove for another day or what seemed like another day until she began to hallucinate and heard her own voice raised in grief and wonder in the car so she stopped at a motel just off the interstate highway where she couldn't sleep moving about the room in the semidark—she had kept the bathroom light on, and the door just slightly ajar—and lying on top of the corduroy bedspread that smelled like stale smoke and hair oil and then something, some presence, in the room woke her at dawn (though dawn was still dark), teeth chattering with cold, Is that you Daddy? Daddy is that you?—and her shaking fingers switched on the light and of course she was alone.

At the hospital the next morning at 10:15 she went directly to the

fifth floor where her father had a private room and there was the
woman who was her stepmother waiting for her, waiting to hug her
in an embrace that hurt, beginning to choke and cry, It's bad, this
woman was saying, and Try not to excite him, please, this woman was
saying, and her nostrils contracted from the woman's perfumy smell,
Oh no you don't, she was thinking, smiling where the woman
couldn't see, you don't seduce this baby, oh no. These were not her
words precisely nor was their cadence hers but she had no time to
consider the strangeness of it, and at her father's bedside too she was
in control speaking calmly and lucidly not about to break down like
her stepmother seeing Daddy's right eye blurred and milky like a
marble egg fixed on some distance beyond her head but the left eye
was Daddy's old good eye shining, wasn't it, with love fierce as hurt.
     They squeezed each other's fingers hard, these two, in code. Oh
they knew each other!—they knew! They whispered so others (in the
corridor outside the room) could not hear. At first she laughed entertaining Daddy with quick-capsule accounts of traveling in Europe,
hotel nights and hotel breakfasts and embassy dinners and limousines
and interviewers and it seemed he listened intently as always smiling
and smirking his old good eye shining with humor and their old
complicity in offhandedness in skepticism regarding all that was not,
you might say, them; the two of them; the one that the two of them
became, at such times; when they were together, that is; and others,
though close (in the corridor outside the room, for instance), ex-
cluded. She was gay and witty and entertaining taking no notice of
the plasterish color of Daddy's skin, or the tubes and transparent
things, what snaked into his right forearm at the elbow where it was
bruised and his skinny blue-veined ankle exposed so strangely, you
might almost say luridly, at the corner of the bed, and there was the
catheter in the groin which she could not see and of which she did
not think, nor did she hear the strange labored breathing in the room
nor did she smell the smell in the room that transfixed her nostrils.
Daddy seemed to be asking about Amsterdam wasn't it? or the flight
over the ocean wasn't it? or *her* health—wasn't it? and then he was

trying to explain with the one still-living side of his mouth a way of getting out of, it seemed to be the city, maybe this city or maybe another city, how some people, the word was maybe "citizens" or maybe "civilians," were trapped, but others, the smart ones, had already left taking back-routes and avoiding thoroughfares where they would be picked off from the sky, the sky was the danger Daddy said, or seemed to be saying, plucking at her hand, or trying to pluck at her hand, and she listened and nodded, quickly, avidly, Oh yes. They had to leave at once Daddy said, he'd been a man of power and eloquence and enormous manly charm and just the smallest vein of cruelty in his old life but now his great need his only remaining human need was to make his daughter comprehend the simplest of human truths and she was at his bedside for that purpose. Don't worry she said I know where the border is, we won't be turned back. I don't want to be late he said his good eye spilling tears. She said, We *won't* be late, and so it went there at his bedside where no one else could hear and the words were strange spitty syllables, harsh consonants some would have thought merely sounds, merely sounds and not human sounds at that, and she began to feel the entire right side of her face freeze in its awful grimace and the left side, the still-living side, quiver and ripple like water churning alive with feeding fish with the need to explain, the need to make known all it is you know because this is all that remains of you now, the fiercest most terrible need of all existence and it was there in the room with her like a living thing, a presence, not her father and not herself but born of the conjunction of the two of them for which she'd flown home and driven so many hours and afterward when she was crying angrily and the woman who was her stepmother tried to quiet her, tried to trap her again in that embrace and quiet her she said, He knows what you are planning, she said throwing off the arms, the trap, —he knows, and so do I.

Adultress

She was in love with two men, one of them her husband. The men were approximately the same age, approximately the same height and weight. The lover had graying brown hair with a slight curl, the husband had graying blond hair with a just perceptible wave. One was coiled tight as a spring, the other hummed to himself, absorbed in his own thoughts. She had fallen in love with her lover out of loneliness for the early years of her marriage. She could not recall why she had fallen in love with her husband.

She and her husband had no children but lived in an old spacious house on a street of similar houses. There she arranged her life in a sequence of time slots that dazzled like sheets of plate glass: for adultery involves acrobatic feats, tricks of navigation regarding time, space. The precise relationship of the clock face to the distance that must be traveled. Had she not had her own automobile she could never have become an adultress.

Her lover was separated from his family and lived alone on the twentieth floor of a building that shone in the sun like a Christmas tree ornament. From one wall of windows the river was visible on clear days, from another an expressway cloverleaf. He seemed at times not to know where he was, he kept speaking of home. He was crazy with love for her, he said. He said often. When she came to him his eyes were clear as washed glass with his need for her. Afterward he said, "I hate to be deceiving your husband like this." He said reproachfully, "I hate any kind of deception."

Early in her marriage she and her husband had talked vaguely of having children but for some reason the time for the first baby was never right. Then they went to Europe, traveled by car through the Alps, and when they returned home the talk of children was not resumed. Much of her conversation with her lover had to do with his children. How desperately he loved them, did not want to hurt them. How desperately he wanted to behave in an intelligent and responsible way. His own father, he said bitterly, had been a weak, self-pitying man, prone to histrionic outbursts. Hardly a man at all. "I'd want to kill myself," her lover said passionately, "if I discovered I was turning into him." It was her task and privilege to assure him he was not.

Sleeping with two men left her breathless, giddy. On the edge of euphoria. She wept easily, laughed easily. It was like being in the mountains at twelve thousand feet. The pulse races and careens, the blood thins. She lay in bed with one man, cradling him in her arms, and saw the twists and coils of expressway she would have to navigate to get to the other man, with whom she would also lie in bed, thinking of the return trip. She had memorized most of the exits on the expressway and might have boasted that she could drive the route blindfolded.

The first time she traveled high in the mountains she had not known what was wrong with her—the quickened heartbeat, the rapid shallow breath, the feathery sensation of panic, dread—until someone explained. It's the altitude. It's a touch of altitude sickness. Never fatal, she was told, unless you had cardiac problems.

The love affair continued for months, a year. A year and a half. Her lover pressed her to get a divorce though he and his wife talked occasionally of attempting a reconciliation for the sake of the children. To pacify him she fell in with his plans though if she herself initiated the topic he became upset. Sometimes she invited her lover to parties at her house, or even to small dinners—he was a friend, to a degree, of her husband's, the two men liked each other quite well— but most of the time their love affair was a matter of telephone calls, discreetly placed, and meetings in his apartment or on neutral ground (the palatial new Hyatt Regency, for instance, just off the expressway). Years after the affair was over she would recall the almost unbearable excitement, the apprehension, with which she telephoned her lover, from a pay phone, for instance, in a department store, once from her doctor's office. At such times her hands shook and her throat constricted with the terrible need to cry. I wish I could be with you right now, she would say, and he would say, I wish I could be with you. Sometimes she did cry, and he would console her, soothe her. They would be together after all the next day, most likely. And she knew he loved her, didn't she.

After these telephone calls she felt both exhausted and ecstatic. She might have said that her heart sang, her spirits soared. Her power had been confirmed. Her beauty. It was not so treacherous, sleeping with two men. It would not be fatal.

During much of this time her lover's wife behaved strangely. She took the children away on mysterious trips, she telephoned from distant cities, hinting at danger. She needed money. She needed advice about dental work, schools, household repairs. Sometimes she threatened to do injury, as she put it, to herself and the children.

Her lover telephoned her to speak of these matters, his voice was raw, frantic, sick with guilt. He would dial her number and let the phone ring just once, then hang up; which meant that she should telephone him when she was free to do so. Often she had to wait until her husband was asleep, then she would slip out of the bedroom and dial her lover's number, barefoot and shivering in the kitchen, not having troubled to put on a bathrobe.

Was his wife serious, was it nothing but emotional blackmail, they discussed the subject endlessly. He said again that he wanted to behave decently, intelligently. He wanted to do the right thing if only he knew what the right thing was.

(Once her lover confessed that his wife's violent emotion had always intimidated him. Her passion. Her sexual need. She had seemed to want more, always more, than he could give her, he said, his voice rising with anger. They were in a cool bright airy room on the twenty-third floor of the Hyatt Regency, the filmy white curtains drawn, the air humming from a window unit. "You can't imagine what some women are like," he said. He was stroking her sides, her thighs. Her breasts. She lay with her eyes closed as if asleep. A small heartbeat pulsed in her forehead. "Some women . . . !" he said, his voice trailing off into silence. She did not move, she held herself intact.)

It was not altogether clear when the love affair ended but she thought it must have been when she placed an emergency call to her lover at his office, from an Exxon station on the expressway. She had had a minor accident: a driver passing her carelessly on the right had cut sharply in front of her, she hadn't been able to brake swiftly enough to avoid a collision, she was badly shaken and could not seem to get her breath though no one was injured and the accident was assuredly not her fault. She was being punished, she thought. Her mind had wandered and she was being punished even if the accident hadn't been her fault.

Her car was towed to the Exxon station and she telephoned her lover at once. She telephoned her lover before she telephoned her husband. What if she had been injured, she said. What if she had been hospitalized. What would they do, she said. What would they do.

Her lover was distracted, upset. He commiserated with her. But she wasn't hurt, was she?—and the car wasn't badly damaged?

"But what would we do," she said, beginning to cry, "if one of us was hospitalized. If one of us died."

She could hear her voice rising in hysteria but she could not control it. Even the fact that people in the service station could overhear her seemed to make no difference. Her eyes welled with tears, her face burned. She was saying, "What would we do, what would we do," again and again, helplessly, "what if one of us died," her breath came in harsh stinging slivers like slivers of glass though she was not injured, she hadn't even struck her forehead on the windshield or been thrown against the steering wheel.

Then she was saying, "I don't want to live like this, I want to die."

Her lover spoke reasonably, calmly. He pointed out that she had had a shock and she must telephone her husband at once and tell him what had happened. She should take a taxi home. She should see a doctor. Surely she wasn't injured but she had suffered a shock and should see a doctor as soon as possible, did she understand? It did no good to get hysterical.

She understood.

She and her husband met her lover for drinks at a downtown hotel. The occasion was casual, her lover's birthday perhaps. They would order a bottle of champagne, they would sit and chat for an hour. It seemed to be so rare, her husband said, that the three of them saw one another.

When she was alone with her husband she thought of her lover and when she was alone with her lover she thought of her husband but now that she was seated at a small table with both men her mind wandered and lost itself amidst the gentle silvery tinkling of a water-fall close by. The cocktail lounge was situated at the base of an atrium that rose for a dozen floors; it was lavishly decorated with mosaics in jade, emerald, and gold, and potted orange trees, and tall narrow strips of mirrored glass.

She had a glass of champagne, and then another. Her husband and

her lover were talking about a mutual acquaintance who was ru-
mored to be close to bankruptcy. Her lover would not look at her;
he sat tense and unnaturally straight in his chair, looking at her
husband. Both men were eating Brazil nuts out of a little glass bowl.
She excused herself and went to the ladies' room, some distance
away. The carpet was so thick, so new, her heels sank in it. The air
hummed and smelled of a slightly acidic spray perfume. She saw her
mirrored reflection, that grim gloating sallow face, the too-dark lipstick she supposed fashionable, the limp fading hair that had been cut
the day before. Beautiful, one of them had said of her, stroking her
belly, her breasts, framing her face in his hands, or had it been both
men? and when? She wasn't drunk and she wasn't hysterical but she
ran cold water to splash onto her wrists. She soaked paper towels,
pressed them against her forehead and that throbbing artery in her
throat. Her lover was now telling her husband that he loved her and
wanted to marry her. His voice was faltering, brave. He had not
wanted to hurt anyone and he had not wanted to deceive anyone but
somehow it had happened. He hated deception. He wanted to behave
decently and responsibly. But he was in love, in love. And it was
necessary to . . .

She was drying her face, slapping at her cheeks. Her eyes shone
with a steely triumph. She smeared dark lipstick on her mouth and
blotted it savagely and rather liked the effect, there *was* something
savage about her, a woman with a long history of deceit, an adultress.
A pretty fluffy jewel-laden woman of late middle age entered the
powder room, stooped a little to regard her in the mirror, giggled,
cried out in a sweet drunken Virginia drawl, "Now *there's* a happy
girl," the remark was not at all rude, it seemed quite the right thing,
the necessary thing. Yet a moment later the older woman tripped and
fell heavily, uttering a wild little scream.

She turned at once from the mirror and tried to help the woman
to her feet. Drunk! A drunkard! In fact she had been uneasily aware
of the woman in the cocktail lounge, seated at a table near her own
with an elderly gentleman and a loud-voiced younger man, their son

perhaps. While her husband and her lover talked she had observed
that filmy floating bleached hair, impeccably styled, the pale pow-
dered skin, the restless eyes, the wink of diamonds on thin trembling
fingers. The woman wore a lacy ruffled white pants suit that would
have looked ludicrous on most women her age. And high-heeled
sling-back open-toed white kidskin Italian sandals. And beneath her
elaborate makeup mask she was a beautiful woman, still, or would
surely have been, were she not now suddenly stricken by a spasm of
vomiting.

Her husband and her lover seemed to be waiting for her, had she
been gone that long? Ten minutes. Fifteen. But they were smiling
too. They had devoured all the Brazil nuts, the waitress was bringing a fresh bowl. Should they order a second bottle of champagne?
What did she think? Both men stood in deference to her, or,
rather, made motions at standing, her lover in awkward haste, her
husband more mechanically, pulling her flimsy wire-backed chair
away from the table so that she could sit. What had they been
talking about, she asked, what had she missed, and they said
they'd been talking about, well what *had* they been talking
about?—one thing or another. But why had she been gone so long,
her husband asked, and she said with a pretty shrug of one shoulder, "There was a sick woman in the ladies' room, I couldn't just
leave her."

Superstitious

She knew she was in love, he was the person she thought about, obsessively, even when she believed she wasn't thinking of anyone or anything at all. At night when she slept alone, which was most nights; during the day when she made her way like a sleepwalker through a delicate equilibrium of forces,—benevolent forces, dangerous forces, tugs and swerves and unexpected careenings of good and bad luck. If she did things right he would love her, if she did things wrong he would stop loving her, the universe was as simple and as terrible as that: the truth we've always known.

She had always had a strong personality but that counted for very little now. Now she was fighting for her life. She wore her grandmother's opal ring for good luck, and the little jade cross on a gold chain (or, if she didn't wear the cross, she was obliged to keep it lying on her bureau top, chain outspread as if it were on display). She placated danger by being friendly to people in stores, to strangers on the street; she never drove more than five miles an hour above the speed limit; never behaved aggressively. (If she was too transparently good, however, the stratagem might work against her. Hypocrite, she sometimes thought in disgust, —who do you think you're deceiving? *Him?*) At night in her bed she always lay on her back, arms crossed to hug herself tight, to keep herself still, hardly moving all night long except to pull her nightgown away where it stuck against her damp skin. It was important that she use cups and plates and glasses that weren't cracked, or chipped; if the telephone rang she never answered before the third or fourth ring because if she did it wouldn't be him. Most of the days of the week, except Fridays, were neutral, which meant they could suddenly swing in any direction, but Saturdays were generally good days and Sundays, like Fridays, were generally bad. Bad days meant that she had to be extremely careful not only with her actions—finishing every task she began, for instance, counting up items methodically—but with her thoughts. Selfish thoughts were dangerous, wicked thoughts were dangerous, but overly optimistic thoughts were dangerous too. She never dared to sing aloud, even to hum under her breath, on a bad day: that was tempting disaster.

Her lover had a heavy, handsome face, dark glistening eyes, dark eyebrows with a ridge of bone. His hair was thinning at the crown of his head but worn rather long, covering the tips of his ears. He drove a little white Mercedes convertible coupe, his work, as he said, had to do with "finances," he had a fifth-degree black belt in karate, he was either divorced or separated from a woman who was either his second or his third wife and who lived in another city. When they were together he sometimes looked at her as if he were dreaming with his eyes open and she was in the dream—she *was* the dream. When they were together, alone, he always behaved like a gentleman, he said wise, witty, funny things, everything was harmonious, dazzling-warm sunshine, a pulse beating strong and hopeful in the wrist, kisses, caresses, fingers clasped just so, the passenger's door of the little white coupe closed just so, she knew she was in love without needing to say the words and without being told that she was loved in turn. Afterward, however, when he was gone, she heard things he said and they didn't sound right. She saw his eyes again, and his mouth, a way he had of smiling with half his mouth, and none of it seemed right. She began to be frightened, she knew that her bad luck was swinging against her for wanting him too much when he didn't want her.

Sometimes they made love in her house, in her bed, and sometimes he forgot to touch her, as if his thoughts had drifted loose and she was merely a presence, a face, a voice, he happened to be with, no one whose name mattered. When they did make love she lost herself almost immediately in sensation, her personality drained away, her eyes rolled back in her head, she cried out with love, she gave herself up to love, it was only afterward that she began to feel uneasy: it might be the next morning, it might be a day or two later: suddenly she would see his face again, his tight mean mocking expression, she would feel him gripping her breasts or her thighs and this time it would hurt, and if she checked she might discover a few bruises, welts in the soft pale flesh. Gradually it occurred to her that there were two men, two lovers—the one she was with, the one she looked at, and talked to, and made love with, and another man, the actual man, whom she never saw at all but could only imagine when she was alone.

It was strange, she thought, how she could start out as a certain person with him, at the beginning of the evening, but by the end of the evening she'd be somebody else, pulled apart in clumps and pieces, like a jigsaw puzzle. She loved him too much, she deserved to be punished, long ago she'd been warned against giving herself away too cheaply, she knew what that meant, didn't she, men never respected women who did certain things, no they never respected them no matter what they or anyone else said: the truth we've always known.

He went away, he seemed to have forgotten her, the days of good luck merged with the days of bad luck as clean water is defiled by muddy water, easing together. Now her fastidious little rituals were exposed as silly tricks (smiling in the stores until her mouth ached, looking strangers full in the face to show how her eyes were dry and clear), it couldn't matter less which cup she drank from, which plates and silver she used, whether she brushed her hair an even number of strokes (which was "good" luck) or an odd number (which was "bad"). He telephoned her once but made no promises. In her agitation she barely recognized his voice. Was he thousands of miles away, or calling from a local pay phone? After they hung up she began crying though she'd been lighthearted enough on the telephone, she was lighthearted most of the time, in fact, making people happy is a way of being made happy, she'd understood that long ago. She cried intermittently for days and sometimes she seemed to hear the telephone ringing again, in the midst of her tears, but if she stopped and listened hard it didn't ring, but in her mind it was ringing and she concentrated hard on picking up the receiver and now he was saying he regretted going away, he really did love her, could he drop by that evening, and she stopped breathing, it was so real, she felt almost happy thinking about it, but of course the telephone wasn't ringing and if, later in the day, it did ring, it would not be him.

He went away, he must have forgotten her, but then one night he telephoned again and wanted to see her,—he wanted to make love again, didn't she want it too?—and she felt dizzy with the heat of his skin, she felt his moist quick breath, she shut her eyes and he was already in the room with her, she was laughing and saying, Yes, oh yes, to prove that she hadn't despaired, she hadn't stopped believing in him and in their love. Suddenly she remembered how he would poke his tongue in her ear, teasing, tickling, how he would suck at her earlobes, her nipples, even her toes, sometimes hurting her, but in the next instant she forgot what she was thinking of, so it *was* love, she'd been waiting for him all along.

I want you, he said, I want to make love to you, he said, don't you want it too? and she felt weak, a little sick, as if someone was pressing on her chest with the flat of his hand. She didn't know what to say, which words to voice, to please him most.

One night he took her driving up in the mountains, he insisted she sit close to him so that he could clasp her left hand in his right hand and from time to time squeeze her thigh, he was crazy about her, he said, he couldn't get enough of her, he said, she wasn't drunk but she began to giggle, she was flying high, a nice warm buzz to the back of the skull, all she'd prayed for and maneuvered for, making her way through that treacherous equilibrium of forces, desperate for love, haphazard as milkweed pollen blown in the wind, she was wearing the opal ring edged with tiny diamonds, she was wearing the jade cross hidden inside her clothes, if he'd hurt her when they made love he hadn't meant it, very likely he hadn't even noticed which meant it wasn't deliberate, it was never deliberate, except possibly as a test of some kind. For a long time they drove in silence, snaking their way through the foothills, up into the mountains, a good-luck moon sailing through the clouds, his warm dry steely fingers linked with hers, he said softly, "I know what you're thinking," but it wasn't a question she had to answer, she had only to sit there, close beside him, staring smiling at the narrow road that curved before them in the headlights. He was kneading her thigh through her dress and she held herself steady, she held herself worthy, waiting for what he might say next.

That afternoon she'd wandered into the children's zoo near the shopping center, she found herself standing by a wire cage for birds, about twelve feet across, admiring the birds, at least at first she was admiring them, and then she was compulsively counting them to make sure she had taken note of them all—a single peacock, three mourning doves, two bantam roosters, a duck with frayed-looking feathers, another duck, another mourning dove, or was it a pigeon, nine birds, she'd been about to leave when by the merest chance she glanced up at the roof of the cage and saw two more birds, mourning doves or pigeons: she had almost missed them, she was getting that careless. For a long while she stood there, trembling, her fingers caught in the wire mesh, not trusting herself to move away.

A Sentimental
Encounter

Those days, radiant and shimmering with fluorescent light, when she rarely required sleep. Small sinewy knots in her blood, passing with difficulty through her heart, kept her alert; there was never a time when she couldn't have stammered out her name and her purpose for existing. She first hated, then loved, the smell of old books, the fact of so many books in languages no one expected her to understand. The red-glowing exit sign that took on many meanings. The hum of the secret ventilators. Whisperings, gigglings, clumsy love-encounters behind tall banks of books: undergraduates brash and innocent as puppies. She was a scholar at a great university but she doled out rewards to herself like a skeptical Momma doling out sweets on a plate, You *know* you don't deserve this but . . . Running breathless down a half-dozen flights of stairs from the fifth floor to C-level where the ventilators really hummed and throbbed, you knew you were near to the heart of it now, felt the excitement, the giddy dread. The underground vending machine room smelling of cigarette smoke, spilled coffee, a day's accumulation of stubbed-out butts, crumpled napkins, the fat boy's perspiration, the greasy clotted hair of the girl with the blemished face. There was a subtle sweetly rancid odor about the Indian student, a young man with beautiful startled eyes who sometimes stared at C. though this was a place where no one stared or spoke or smiled, this was a place of refuge and utter aloneness, the solace of sticky-topped tables, a clock with a glaring face whose black hands could be seen to move if you stared hard enough. The machines winked and vibrated, their colored lights—red, green, amber—hinted at enormous solitary pleasures, secret delights. It was her strategy to enter with her head lowered looking at no one but quick to see if anyone had taken her table in the farthest corner, her heart gave a mean little twist if anyone had dared.

There she was invisible since no one came into the room except strangers. There she could work for hours, from mid-afternoon until the library closed at midnight, taking meticulous notes from over-sized books, drinking coffee that stirred her blood, sometimes if she was desperately hungry eating potato chips one at a time, half shame-fully, her nerves strung tight at the noise of the rattling cellophane wrapper she could never outwit. If she wanted she could lay her head on her arms not to sleep but to calm her thoughts, she might see a skier plunging down a glaring-white mountainside, she held her breath at the grace, the risk, it was no one she knew, sometimes she was startled to see a waterfall so close, white dazzling cascading water, she waited for a human figure to appear but none did. . . . Sometimes she was the only person in the vending room but that was a rare privilege. In late afternoon it was crowded, after nine o'clock in the evening there were only the strangers whom she came to recognize and even to know without ever looking at them, they were the ones who respected others' privacy, always sitting at empty tables, sitting with their backs to one another if it was possible, keeping very still. They never spoke to anyone, perhaps because there was nothing to say. They never sat at her table even if no empty table was availa-ble, like her they'd mastered the strategy of looking into the room from the doorway and quickly retreating if the circumstances were infelicitous, if for instance a noisy clump of undergraduates had gathered at one of the tables, talking and smoking, laughing, flirting, or if the elderly skeletal ex-professor of Slavic Languages was there, drinking sweetened coffee and sucking at an unlit pipe and boyishly eager for someone to talk with, anyone would do, even C. who so clearly hadn't time, even the fat boy with the wheezing breath and the odd jerky uncoordinated movements who knew how to be rude if rudeness was required.

Weeks and months, hours when the clock hand froze to the enormous white face, then sprang slyly forward, the hum, the vibration, the machines deep in the bowels of the earth, a smell of stale cigarette smoke and stale unwashed flesh, not her own, well perhaps it was her own, she hadn't time for the personal bodily life, she hadn't time to think of physical matters, she was after all a highly regarded young scholar with an infinity of work ahead and a finite quantity of time. One page followed another, one book seamlessly followed another, there was the taking of meticulous and very possibly pointless notes in a schoolgirl hand which had always pleased her elementary school teachers but which she knew to be, in secret, not hers. Weeks and months, an autumn and a winter and a dull gray rainy spring, she came to know the pale fat boy well without ever needing to look directly at his face, she came to know the girl with the blemished skin who was studying German and who drank can after can of Coca-Cola, there was the olive-skinned Indian student in his perfectly ironed white shirts and his silky dark maroon turban, eyes quick and fleeting as small fish, smile bent and wistful, a curious compulsive taste for Orange Crush (a bright drink whose cans carried the tiny legend, or warning, *This product contains no fruit juice*) . . . and there was also, less frequently, a blond bearded graduate student in mathematics who was capable of sitting motionless for long periods of time staring at the concrete wall a few feet away . . . and a very black, very restless young African who slammed at the vending machines if they swallowed up his money or lit up with EMPTY beside the items he punched, and who disappeared over Christmas break and never returned. C. had hated him but she also missed him. She dreamt of the vending machine room empty of her, her privileged table in the corner empty, and wondered what that might mean.

One night the fat boy began to whisper and laugh to himself, he dropped coins in one vending machine after another, he hurried out into the stairwell to devour his food in private, ice cream sandwich, potato chips, can of Coca-Cola, can of 7-Up, one and two and three candy bars, yes he knew they were watching, yes he knew they were counting, they were waiting for him to hurry up the stairs and disappear but he wouldn't hurry up the stairs and disappear, he simply stepped into the stairwell to devour his food, then he came back panting into the room and dropped more coins into the machines, his face was white and glazed and flaccid, his eyes defiant, C. could see the madness radiant about him though she sat with her head bowed and her eyes fixed on the page before her, she could hear her frightened voice, *Is something wrong? Is there anything I can do?* though in fact she sat absolutely still and would not glance up and would not flee from the room as, one by one, others were doing.

Minutes passed, and the siege continued, the fat boy knew he had them cowering, he knew he had them cornered, at last only C. and the Indian student remained, C. hunched trembling over her books, the Indian student openly staring, for there is something sacred about madness, a stranger's madness at least.

But the siege, begun at approximately 10:10 P.M., ended abruptly at 10:30 P.M. when the fat boy's footsteps pounded heavily on the stairs, and C. and the Indian student were left alone, suddenly alone, and he turned to look at her, and she lifted her eyes to his, and they smiled, stricken, relieved, gripped by a queer hilarity, and then he gathered up his books and left the room but C. had the idea he hadn't really left, he was going to wait for her, on the landing perhaps, on B-level perhaps, in that shadowy alcove by the photostat machine. . . . She tasted both panic and exhilaration but couldn't have known if it was the fat boy's or her own.

So she wasn't surprised but she was a little apprehensive when he did appear out of the shadows of the deserted B-level, waiting giddy and drunken as she, sweating with excitement, it was now 10:35 P.M. and they had a good deal of time before the library closed, a luxurious amount of time, still he was quick, ravenous, the white, white teeth bared in a smile she seemed to know very well, the dark skin giving off heat, she felt a spiky little knot jerk its way through her heart but she made no resistance, yielded wordless and impatient as he, mouths hard and swift, tongues probing, for who would know, who would be a witness, she tasted panic at the back of her mouth but her arms were around him, her nails digging into the crisp fabric of his shirt, she smelled hair oil, something dark and sweet and faintly rancid, she'd been smelling it for weeks, watching the sly insolent eyes moving onto her, the olive-dark skin burning like her own, what joy, what delight, a giddy maniacal lust as urgent as her own most secret wish, not to be resisted (for he was strong, he was capable, despite his slender build—he wasn't to be trifled with either) should she have wished to resist and in fact she did not, it was far too late for resistance.

Of course they never met again, never even learned each other's name.

Forever after she avoided the vending machine room, rarely ventured below-ground in the great library, learned to turn quickly away when she glimpsed a man, any man, olive-skinned, or wearing a turban. She avoided too any plump youngish man who might turn into the fat boy.

It was the boy she dreamt of, not her Indian lover, a white radiant face, eyes sly and knowing, the sliver in the heart, the quick hot stare of recognition.

Señorita

He had a heart attack a few weeks after his fifty-third birthday, not a severe one. In the hospital and, later, at home, convalescing, he fell to dreaming, couldn't seem to help himself, dozing off with a book on his lap, a sheaf of computer printouts from his investment broker, suddenly it was forty years ago, he saw with a remarkable vividness his young cousin Vic's car, the stripped-down Studebaker Hawk, rusted, bronze, splendid, with red zigzag lightning strokes inexpertly painted on its sides. He saw Vic with his sideburns and slow cynical grin. He saw himself, skinny, ferret-faced, dark, a blurred figure as in a photograph where inconsequential figures are not brought into focus—himself, seated beside Vic in the Studebaker. He'd been fifteen and Vic was only a year or two older when Vic drove him downtown, far downtown, to South Main Street and Waterman Street, where the burlesque houses were located.

Don't you tell your parents about this, Vic said.

The Rialto, the Follies Burlesque, the old RKO Palace, art deco exterior gone shabby, enormous marquee held up by cables. There were posters, blown-up photographs, Satin Doll fondling her swollen breasts, Lana X sultry, platinum blond, eyes nearly closed and lips lewdly pursed, the incomparable Lily St. Cyr in her bubble bath, Gypsy Rose Lee with head flung back, Señorita Carmen with dead-white skin, fleshy crimson mouth, cascading black hair, the eyes sullen and defiant, Oh God what beauty, and so on display! He was faint with astonishment, the violent stirring of desire. One afternoon, cruising the street in the Studebaker, they saw three burlesque dancers leaving a White Tower restaurant, tall leggy women in spike heels, gaudy fake-fur coats swinging open, teased hair, faces bright with makeup, they were laughing together oblivious of passersby who stared and of the boys in the bronze Studebaker Hawk. Oh Jesus kid just look, Vic said, elated, angry, pounding the steering wheel with his fists, I mean just *look*.

A year or so later, using his older brother's ID, he went to a show at the Palace without telling Vic, without telling anyone, nearly sick with excitement and dread, sitting by himself near a side aisle, head down at first, shoulders slouched, he was in terror that someone might recognize him and call out his name. But the show, the spectacle, had nothing to do with him, rolled right over him, astonishing, heart-stopping, a chorus of women clattering on spike heels, shaking their breasts, their rears, a striptease routine to the tune of "Stormy Weather," black textured stockings, platinum hair piled and coiled and threaded with rhinestones, the balloon breasts, plump quivering buttocks, long long legs muscled at the calf and softer above the knee, a sudden drum roll, the climbing and teasing of a saxophone, the woman's breasts nearly naked except for glittering patches of cloth over her nipples, and now the pumping of the groin, the sudden wild ecstatic pumping and thrusting of the groin, a sight he couldn't believe, a terrible paralyzing beat he couldn't endure, he had to close his eyes, he had to hide his face in his hands, shame, exultation, the most powerful pangs of desire, he sat soaked in perspiration until the routine was over, the men had finished applauding and stamping their feet, and a comic in a beret and monocle, a foolish-looking old man, poked his head and shoulders through the curtain. Youse callin' my name? the comic cried in a falsetto Brooklyn accent.

He returned to the Palace another time, and another, a half-dozen times in all, he went once to the higher-priced Rialto to see a stripper billed as "Marilyn Mmmmm!," he was entranced by the kittenish Satin Doll, and by the light-skinned Negro Sultana, most of all by beautiful Señorita Carmen with her thick black eyelashes, her yards of black lace and gauze, flawless marble-white skin, her castanets, crashing heels, arrogant queenly manner even as she stripped down to garter belt, stockings, tiny peek-a-boo black lace bikini, black-glittering pasties. Only once did he make the mistake of going to the shabby Follies Burlesque where the dancers, already part unclothed, trotted clattering and squealing on a runway out into the audience— the Follies Burlesque was so small, the seats so cramped, the strippers could look boldly into the faces of the men if they chose, it was all too close, unendurable. The spotlights showed too much, the high heels were deafening, he could even smell the women—perfume, sweat. And only once did he make the mistake of going to a movie house along the strip. He left a half-hour into the first feature of a double billing, in a fever of shock and indignation, he was furious, he'd been cheated, he hadn't paid to see men, he wanted only to see women, beautiful women.

His first semester at college he went once, alone, to a burlesque house a few miles from campus. After that he lost interest. He'd outgrown it. He had better things to do. He thought it was all fairly silly, juvenile. He lost contact with his cousin Vic, who'd joined the Marines and fought in Korea and eventually came back home and got married and had several children and got divorced and went out to the state of Washington to go into a business partnership with a friend and died there, drunk driving it was thought though his family would never admit it.

The heart attack had been a warning, his doctor said. He decided to interpret it that way.

A few weeks after he returned to work he made the drive to a nearby city where there was a meager red-light district of sorts, a few squalid blocks of movie houses, adult bookshops, massage parlors, topless bars. He was curious, that was all. It really meant nothing: it was a diversion.

During his convalescence he'd read a good many books, among them a memoir of Einstein's, and he was haunted by certain statements of Einstein's which struck him as riddles though he supposed they were simply literal, self-evident. *Space is not merely a background for events but possesses an autonomous structure.* What did that mean, he wondered. Could it pertain to a man's life as well as to the physical world . . . ? He knew of gaps in his life, inconsistencies, contradictions, silent spaces stretched over the years, but he didn't know what the gaps might mean or if they meant anything. It was enough to live, he supposed. It would have to be enough.

He was amused, faintly repulsed, only intermittently intrigued by the lurid movie marquees, the posters for Girls Girls Girls, X-Rated Nude Entertainment, *Topless Go-Go*, 24-Hour Red-Hot Massage. The big old theaters were gone forever, these places were merely stores, small tawdry shops along a strip of derelict buildings, weedy vacant lots, cracked pavement. Boutiques selling "sexy" clothing, "sex equipment." A bookshop specializing in "gay sex."

Still, he was curious. It was all innocent, experimental. And it had nothing to do with him.

He looked into the narrow window of the Danish Sex Boutique, he browsed for a half-hour in one of the adult bookshops, one evening he paid five dollars to enter a striptease "palace" that must have seated no more than fifty people at its capacity. There were fewer than twenty patrons scattered amidst the folding chairs, several young women sitting together, talking loudly, laughing, cheering drunkenly throughout most of the show, while the men sat silent and embarrassed. The entertainment was crude, noisy, campy. Women ranging in ages from eighteen to as old as forty danced, kicked, strutted, cavorted, mugged, writhed, stripped virtually naked with very little hesitation, even simulated crude sex play with one another, accompanied not by live musicians but by a badly scratched tape. Sitting at the rear of the little theater he felt his old excitement wash over him nonetheless, that sense of shame, privilege, trespass, extreme personal risk. It had to do with the colored lights, perhaps, with the thumping grinding blues music, the wail of the saxophone and the rolling drum crescendo, as much as it had to do with the women on display. . . . But some of the women were beautiful, he had to admit. Yes they were beautiful. And they knew it, they knew it, strutting and clowning and jiggling their breasts and their asses, even spreading their legs for quick silky gauzy peeks, they knew they were beauties, they knew their power, he sat sweating and clapping, fully given over to their tricks. The ticket had cost only five dollars after all, the show lasted hardly more than an hour, his wife, his family, no one from his legitimate life would ever know, nothing was lost.

Another evening he paid eight dollars for a ticket to Le Cabaret where the strippers were more professional, elaborately made up, cleverly costumed, even the spotlights were skillfully manipulated; the place was a former movie house with real seats. He felt reassured, excited, at once, it was as if he were being placated for all he had endured. The music was live, loud, a saxophone, a bass, drums, electric guitar, the crowd was noisy but attentive, Linda Loveless, Toothy Thorne, Sheena Queen of the Wild, Molly O!, Inez the Hot-Blooded Señorita, big strapping girls with wildly painted eyes, dark rouge, tumbling hair, warm bronze oiled flesh, powerfully muscled legs, thighs, stomachs, shoulders. . . . He was amused, detached, this *was* only amusement, yet he sat in a trance of near-ecstasy as tall beautiful white-skinned Inez stripped and rolled on the floor moaning, grinding, convulsed as if by rapid stabs of electricity, her astonishing long hair flying about her, the saxophone climbing, climbing, an unendurable feat. It was all, he thought, unnervingly realistic. Maybe, he thought, it was real.

Less satisfying was a lunchtime visit to a topless go-go bar where the girls danced listless and perspiring above patrons who took only intermittent interest in them. Girls in their twenties, clearly amateurs, gyrating, bouncing, wriggling to loud rock music piped in overhead, bare exposed breasts, beads and chains around their necks, mock-coyness, mock-passion, even a bit of mock-frenzy though no one took much notice. He felt sorry for them, not at all aroused, one was a girl with an anxious smiling face and honey-brown hair very like his younger daughter's, another was a black girl with rather thick legs, too-heavy breasts, Afro-style hair in a smoky cloud about her face, rich dark skin lightly coated with sweat, oil. Because the dancers were already stripped above the waist and would not remove their tiny bikini panties there seemed little purpose to the odd spectacle, near-naked females mechanically dancing on a small platform raised above the bar amidst noise and drifting clouds of smoke. . . .

He did feel sorry for them, he seemed to be the only man at the bar who watched them with sympathy and concern, so it was unjust, it was certainly something of a shock, when the black girl, covertly scanning the faces below her, stared at him with an expression of angry contempt. No it was hatred, it was savage loathing, she wished him dead where he stood, but in the next instant she looked away, looked down, thick muscled legs moving to the beat, the beat, the blood-heavy lurid beat, her face hard and set, masked, very dark.

In the lavatory he suffered a spell of dizziness, sudden nausea, his head was swimming, he'd had too much to drink too rapidly, wasn't accustomed to alcohol at this time of day. He felt his heart kick, in terror he felt his heart miss a beat, there was something tightening around his chest, yes it was happening, no it could not possibly happen, not here, not in this filthy place, not now. And he ran cold water and splashed it on his face and eventually, after a few minutes, during which time other patrons scrupulously avoided him, after a few panicked minutes the spell lifted and he was himself again.

And what had his visits to the strip to do with his wife, his three children, his business associates, his rather wide circle of friends and acquaintances . . . ? Nothing at all.

Nothing, he thought. They hadn't even any relationship to him.

He returned to Le Cabaret, rather boldly made a date by way of the manager with the stripper who was billed as Inez, just for coffee, afterward, at a Holiday Inn twenty-four-hour coffee shop a mile away. She didn't want anything to drink, she said. She was on pills to keep her weight down and her doctor warned her never to mix alcohol with these particular pills, especially if she was going to drive at night.

Do you have to drive alone? he asked, surprised.

Sure, she said, how else am I going to get home?

Close up the girl was still attractive though her stark black hair was obviously dyed and her skin appeared blemished beneath the crusty Pan-Cake makeup. There were faintly discolored crosshatched circles beneath her eyes, her bright red lipstick was smeared. She exuded a smell of heat, of stale perfumy flesh; she seemed nervous, allowing him to help her take off her suede coat, then insisting upon sitting with it draped over her shoulders in the narrow booth. She was cold, she said. Underneath her nail polish her nails were probably blue. Did he know what that meant? she asked.

No, he said, puzzled.

Low blood pressure, she said. The coat had a fluffy bright-dyed rabbit fur collar which she pulled against her neck as if for warmth.

She smoked a cigarette, sipped at her cup of coffee, seemed awkward, amused, not quite meeting his eye. He did feel like a fool though the meeting was intended only to be casual, he was only curious about her life, sultry "Señorita Inez"—whose name, she quickly told him, was really Rose Ann. She wasn't Spanish either, she was Italian, sort of, her mother's side of the family.

She couldn't stay long, she said. Her eleven-year-old was taking care of her six-year-old and that always made her nervous. You got kids? she asked him suddenly, squinting through the smoke from her cigarette.

He told her he admired her dancing, she was so beautiful, she was by far the best of the performers at the Cabaret, and she said, curtly, as if he'd offended her, Okay thanks, mister. Then she said, frowning,

The other girls are pretty good too—we learn from each other, help each other out. Molly, y'know, the redhead, she's the oldest, she's actually the best if you know the basic routines, I mean how they're supposed to go. She's the nicest too. Lent me shoes when I first got started. Makeup. Money.

He asked how she'd begun her career. She said, Career?—squinting at him as if she thought he was mocking her. Shit, she said, I just drifted into it like anybody else. First you're a waitress or something, then a better job opens up, you take what comes along. With me, my marriage broke up and I was stuck, you know?—so I had to get hustling. My mother helped me out for a while but there wasn't all that much she could do. Then she didn't like my boyfriends coming around, we had all these fights and who needs it?

He asked what sort of training she'd had, what was her professional background, if any, and she seemed not to hear. She said, Also I wanted to get away from where I was living. My ex-husband kept telephoning, dropping by. Sometimes he'd telephone and hang up but I knew who it was. I told him I'd call the police and he said, Go ahead. They take one look at you and they know who they're dealing with, go ahead.

He said that was too bad, he was sorry to hear it. Was her husband giving her trouble now?

No, she said, stubbing out her cigarette in an ashtray, —'cause the fucker doesn't know where I am. Or the kids either.

He asked her again if she'd had any professional training and she said vaguely that she'd had a few lessons from a friend, another stripper, but mainly you learn it pretty fast, it's all sort of natural. Just get up there, the music's going, et cetera. A few times in front of a mirror then that's it, you're ready, she said, smirking, for the big time.

It does seem natural, he said slowly, confused. I mean—the way you do it.

She laughed. In a bantering voice she said, Okay, mister, I read you.

She went on to complain of working conditions at the Cabaret. The rooms backstage never got cleaned unless the girls cleaned them themselves. There were cockroaches big as your fist. There wasn't any real heating. The owners were liars, they'd tell you anything. The manager was a fairy who hated women, and a drunk. When she started she was supposed to get $145 a week plus fifty percent of any tips that came her way but somehow it never worked out to much more than $130 a week. And out of that she had to pay for her costumes, her makeup, her shoes, any food she ate, and so forth. Her feet had gotten two sizes larger, two actual sizes larger, since she'd started dancing, and she could only afford cheap shoes so they were always wearing out. A good pair of shoes, good and strong for dancing, metal-reinforced it's called, she said, lowering her voice, —they cost seventy-five, eighty, you believe it?

He said sympathetically, That's a lot. He cleared his throat, smiled. He said, Maybe I could buy you a pair?—no strings attached or anything.

I don't need charity, she said. I'm not looking for any handouts.

Of course not, would you like me to lend you the money?

Maybe, she said. I don't know.

She seemed pleased, though, placated. He ordered her a second cup of coffee and watched as she expertly ripped open a tiny package of sugar with a talonlike red fingernail. Snuggling inside her coat she said in a husky voice, The thing is, mister, you meet a wide range of people in my line of work, you have to be careful. Not to give out a telephone number or an address, for instance. That's the Cabaret policy actually.

I understand, he said.

The police are always putting on pressure, you know? she said.

Oh yes I understand, he said, feeling suddenly very tired. I can certainly understand.

When they were leaving the Holiday Inn she told him in a confidential tone that the rumor was, the Cabaret owners were mixed up in the rackets, the Mafia. Some kind of squeeze was being put on them. The girls were worried that the place might be firebombed or something. Christ, she said, where'd that leave me if I was onstage at the time?—where'd it leave my kids?

He had to drive her back to the Cabaret, to the parking lot. At her car he thanked her for the pleasant hour, he said he hoped they might see each other again, he talked quickly, confusedly, not entirely certain of what he said. He took out his wallet and gave her several bills, rather carelessly—twenties, a ten—ah, here was a fifty, which should please her—and she thanked him, suddenly rather subdued, embarrassed. Next time you see the show, she said, backing away, be sure to notice the shoes.

He would, he said. He would do that.

He stayed away from Le Cabaret, visited the strip itself only once or twice. Though he was lonely, very lonely. And bitter. And angry. Was it only a matter of money after all, he wondered.

He'd punish the girl by forgetting her. Erasing her from his mind: that was within his power.

"Inez": a curved red-painted fingernail razoring open a cellophane wrapper, a husky insinuating voice. Blemished skin under the heavy makeup. Mister, she'd kept saying. Mister. Like a nudge in the ribs. A certain beat, blood-heavy beat, Mister she'd said, raising her painted eyes to his.

Their conversation in the Holiday Inn coffee shop faded from his memory as completely as if it had been a conversation he'd only happened to overhear, between strangers.

After nearly a year he forced himself to return to Le Cabaret but the girl was no longer there. So far as he knew. At least he didn't recognize her among the performers.

Driving home in a light drizzling rain he was suddenly overcome by a sensation of exhaustion. His eyelids began to close, once or twice the steering wheel swerved. He knew the situation was dangerous, he should pull over to the side of the road and sleep, or stop for coffee, but his wife thought he had been at a business dinner in the city and would be home before midnight, and already it was twelve-thirty; and he was a good twenty miles from home.

He drove at sixty miles an hour, sixty-five, seventy, in an effort to jar himself awake.

The headlights of oncoming traffic blinded him, the double yellow line in the center of the highway slipped in and out of focus. He did not know if he had enjoyed himself this evening—he did not know in what way he might have enjoyed himself—but now he felt cheated, resentful, angry at someone or something without knowing why. He felt dizzy, slightly nauseated; his breath was coming short. Running uphill, pushing his way uphill—always uphill. When his eyelids sank he saw a boy's clenched fists pounding at a steering wheel. Then his eyes snapped open and the highway glared and buzzed with the lights of an oncoming truck. The pavement was slick, the air misty, heavy, difficult to breathe. His windshield was flooded with dirty water as cars swept by him at high speeds. He could not keep up his speed: the effort was too great. Again the wheel swerved and he set it right. He was angry but tired, so very tired, it was unfair, unjust, in a blinding circle of light that broke into numerous agitated circles of light the woman emerged in her yards of black lace, tall black comb holding up her glossy hair, beautiful pale face tilted at a dramatic angle. Now the sharp retort of castanets in her powerful fingers, now the deafening clatter of stiletto heels. The shroud of black lace is being unwound, slowly and teasingly unwound, unwound, to reveal black satin underwear: tight-laced brassiere out of which her enormous white breasts spill, the garter belt, the black fishnet stockings. A tiny cloth rose affixed to the top of one stocking. He sees his young cousin behind the steering wheel of the bronze Studebaker—the red zigzag lightning strokes on its sides. There, beside him, another boy, skinny, dark, leaning far forward, his features too blurred to recognize.

Face

Some of the damned in the neuropsychiatric ward are truly blind and deaf but many of the others rarely trouble to glance up or to listen for what's worth their attention *out there?*—it's *in here* inside their honeycombed heads that fascinates. Old Royal Jake as he's called, the eighty-eight-year-old mnemonist, and J.E. the adolescent confabulator accursed with hypermnesia and chorea who can't stop yammering and twitching, a dozen stroke victims two of which, weirdly twinlike, can see only halves—hemispheres—half their worlds sliced away like you'd slice something coreless, perfectly in two. There are the tumor-ridden spastics whose eyes roll like tiny fruits in a slot machine, there are parkinsonian catatonics who barely shift with the tide. Ahoy! she wants to scream at them in a shrill gay voice. Look at me! Look *out here!* Where are you all hiding!

It is a city of the damned in a vertical prison just off the expressway. The noises of the city thrum through the tall building and through the patients' skulls. As an intern she was duly warned that such disturbances might prove contagious not as diseases are contagious (though she has begun to suspect that that too is a possibility) but by way of psychic osmosis: the malevolent power of turbulent waves in air or water to do violent damage while in themselves invisible, intangible. In her youth of only eight or ten months ago she haughtily refused to listen.

Her face, in consequence, has gradually shrunk—that is, the features of the face, the "distinguishing" features, inside the bland map of flesh. She no longer dares contemplate its ravages in the mirror either at the hospital or at home ("at home" meaning her apartment in a high-rise building near another expressway). One of the aphasiacs (elderly Caucasian, female, also blind) extends a slow tremulous groping hand as if to stroke her face but she shies away in terror of losing, so swiftly, her face.

Nights when she's off duty she drives. Drives her car. Presses her foot on the gas pedal, drives. The air is opaque, the pavement greased. If she looked—which, systematically, she does *not*—she'd see the streets and sidewalks populated by the patients in the neuropsychiatric ward, or their close kin. Gradually the city is filling up with them. With us. She's thinking: No-name and no-face?

In the parking lot there's sure to be a dozen identical cars like hers, in the metallic blue everyone has. Spaced among the other cars so if she's drunk leaving the bar she'll be trying to force her key into a stranger's lock which is always amusing.

Some nights that's all—the only amusement. Others, like tonight,—at first there was nothing and then there turned out to be someone looking at her and by degrees (this might require minutes, or hours) she felt herself begin to revive, the facial mask tingling with sensation. And gradually she sees this person, this woman, this face that's hers, or *her*—like crystals in a magic solution, materializing. Her brain is intact, her speech hers. Her face has not yet been split up the middle.

There, no-name, no-face, he's standing over her as if making his claim. There you are! he says happily.

Or he says, Hey—don't we know each other?

Or, Honey I've been waiting for you a long long time.

August Evening

He drives a new-model metallic-blue Cougar with all the accessories including air conditioning and a tape deck and beige kidskin interior plus some special things of his own for instance a compass affixed to his dashboard, a special blind-spot mirror, extra strips of chrome around the windows and license plates, a glitter-flecked steering wheel "spin," and, in cold weather, a steering wheel covering made of snakeskin. In warm weather he likes to cruise the city as he'd done twenty years ago or maybe more except now he's alone and not with his friends as he'd been back then. As if nothing has changed and the surprise is that not much really has changed in certain parts of the city and off the larger streets and he's drawn back always a little expectant and curious to the old places for instance St. Mary's Church where they'd all gone and the grammar school next door, the half-dozen houses his parents had rented while he and his brothers were growing up though he couldn't name their chronological sequence any longer and one or two of them have been remodeled, glitzy fake-brick siding and big picture windows so it's difficult to recognize the houses except by way of the neighboring houses which are beginning to be unrecognizable too. There's a variety store close by the school hardly changed at all where he parks to get a pack of Luckies and just as he's leaving he runs into this woman Jacky he'd known in high school back before she was married and he was married and she's in tight shorts that show the swell of her buttocks and her small round stomach and a tank-top blouse like a young girl would wear looking good with her fleshy smiling mouth and her eyes shadowed in silvery blue and her legs still long and trim though a little bunchy at the knees. At first it almost seems Jacky doesn't recognize him then of course she does and they get to talking and laughing and it's clear she likes him looking at her like that asking him questions about his job and where is he living now since the divorce and what's his ex-wife doing, and then they get to talking about old friends and high school classmates, guys he hung around with, some of them they haven't seen or heard of in years so you'd wonder are they still alive but better not ask. And gradually they run out of things to say but neither wants to break away just yet they're smiling so hard at each other and standing a little closer than you'd ordinarily stand, Jacky's the kind of woman likes to touch a man's arm when she talks, and he's thinking a thought he's had before and probably she has too that the marriages by now are more or less interchangeable like objects blurring in a rearview mirror as you speed away but also it's the warm lazy air smelling of soft tar from the streets and sirens in the distance or is it a freight train like those childhood sounds you'd hear at night . . . melancholy and sweet-sounding with the power to make your eyes fill with tears. And they see themselves off somewhere hurriedly undressing . . . and the frantic hungry coupling . . . and the orgasm protracted for each as in slow motion . . . and the sweaty stunned aftermath, the valedictory kisses, caresses, stammered words. . . . All that they aren't going to do but they're locked together seeing it and Jacky's eyes look dilated and he's feeling the impact of it as if somebody were pushing hard on his chest with an opened hand so that he almost can't breathe.

Honey was that *sweet* are the words he isn't going to say and Jacky can't think of what to say either so they back off from each other and she says "Take care" and he says "O.K.—you too" and he gets in his car and drives off sad-feeling and excited and eager to be gone all at once—knowing not to bother looking for her in the rearview mirror, he's accelerating so fast.

Picname

Why had she done it . . . drifting off from the others, that afternoon, late summer, and down beyond the edge of the park, down a fairly steep hill—the park's boundary being a crumbling stone wall, waist high—and through the tattered underbrush to a gravel road a quarter-mile below, where, just by accident, or seeming so, a girl she knew from school was bicycling, a girl in her grade but older by a year or two, freckled, mildly cross-eyed, big as a near-grown woman, in soiled cotton slacks and a man's T-shirt in which her breasts swung loose and shadowy, frizzed red hair lifting from her head, and her name was Edith, or was it Ethel, her last name ending in "man," perhaps Biedelman, and this girl invites her to come to her house, it's close by she says, and N. doesn't want to go but there she is following alongside the older girl, at school N. and E. are not friends, in fact N. is wary of E., and of E.'s several brothers, the Biedelmans have a certain reputation in the school and even the teachers are fearful of them, but N., a girl of eleven, isn't thinking *This is an adventure* or *This is something I shouldn't be doing* nor is she, caught up fascinated by E.'s drawling derisive talk (of teachers at the junior high, of certain classmates and even friends of E.'s), thinking of the picnic grove she'd left, wandered off from, her parents and her younger brother, her Aunt Betty, her Uncle Dan, her two young girl cousins, the smells of charcoal smoke and meat on the grill, the loud portable radio tuned to a baseball game, from which, irresponsibly perhaps, she'd drifted off telling no one she was going or in which direction she was going, curious simply to see where the weedy path led down the steep tricky hill, very likely she is thinking nothing clear and distinct and purposeful like *Why am I doing this when I don't want to* and years later, forty, even fifty years later, remembering, she will so vividly see the girl E. (Edith? Ethel? Biedelman?) screwing her face up in an expression of laughing contempt, straddling the bicycle as she walks, to keep pace with N., and the bicycle itself—a boy's bike, badly rusted, fenderless, with high spreading handlebars, a worn red seat, missing spokes—and herself as a girl child-sized beside E.: this memory, visual, photographic, being a memory achieved in a sense from the outside, as if it were nothing of N.'s own.

And then they were approaching the Biedelman house, a shack of a house, tin roof, rutted driveway, front porch heaped with trash, and it's the sort of place where a large dog, maybe a German shepherd, begins barking hysterically and rushes at you, but there is no dog, and there are no cars in the drive, nobody's home E. says letting the bicycle fall on the ground as if, done with it now, she could not foresee ever having need of it again, and E. leads N. into the house, into a slant-roofed shed, a storage area piled with kindling wood and trash, and smelling powerfully of kerosene, windowless but the spaces between the boards emit light, a dreamy rayed light, and in this place E. quickly slams the door shut and latches it and nudges N. in the chest and says, "Now I got you!"—as if this were a children's game, and N. has not quite understood. E. is panting as if with exertion, excited, seemingly happy, but when N. tries to push past her to open the door E. shoves her hard enough to knock her to the ground . . . not floorboards but ground: hard-packed dirt. E. squats in front of the door, E. says, "We're locked in here together, nobody going out and nobody coming in," E. repeats these words several times, rocking slightly from side to side, showing her discolored teeth in a grin that looks friendly, small mismatched eyes gleaming up bright

as pennies, "You know what I could do fuckface?—I could do anything I want to do," her forehead prickled with thought, the startling
wonder of thought, its quicksilver improvised nature. Squatting there
holding N. her prisoner, ham-sized thighs straining the fabric of her
slacks, breasts heavy and hard like a big man's clenched fists, and the
smile, the grin, opening up in satisfaction, and N. is too frightened
to cry or even, initially, to speak, disbelieving, surprised, not knowing
if it is a joke? if it is a trick? if E. means to laugh at her for taking
it seriously? if E. will laugh at her and, next month, in school, tell
others about her and mock her there too?—and for what seems like
a long time though it can have been only minutes the two girls stare
at each other wordless, N.'s small frozen smile mirroring E.'s wide
elastic grin weakly, shamefully, E. thinking hard, her mildly crossed
eyes moving fluidly over N. and over objects in the shed as if, in this
magic space of wonder, of improvisation, she is contemplating the
possibilities that suggest themselves . . . dreamlike in seeming of their
own volition to suggest themselves. For instance the long-handled ax
fallen atop a pile of wood, its blade dull-looking but a blade. For
instance the rusted tools, claw-headed hammer, screw driver, hand-
saw, five-foot saw, scattered amid the debris. There is a broken baby
buggy, there are rubber buckle-fronted boots, oil-soaked rags, dis-
carded clothing, over all the stench of kerosene, dirt, cooking odors,
wood smoke, and N. is saying she wants to leave, not quite pleading,
begging, and E. says carefully as if these words were an incantation,
"Nobody going out and nobody coming in," and N. whispers, *"Why
. . . ?"* though knowing there can be no answer. N. is badly frightened
now, bowels contracting with the need to urinate, a convulsive tremor
in her limbs, and how many minutes pass she doesn't know, cannot
gauge, while E., a massive child, holds her prisoner, rocking slightly
from side to side balanced on her heels, her muscular haunches, face
slick with sweat, the corners of her mouth curling upward in intense
surprised innocent pleasure, "You think you're so smart fuckface
don't you, think you, you and them others, are so goddamn fucking
smart don't you, you and them others," even as N. is shaking her

head no, whispering no, she wants to leave she says, her parents will be looking for her she says, they'll call the police if they can't find her she says, and E. repeats, *"Nobody going out and nobody coming in,"* and beneath her voice there is no sound, no sounds, only silence, an absolute terrifying silence, as when N. presses the palms of her hands against her ears praying to God hoping to hear God's voice in reply, except now the silence is heavy and palpable as a wall of water pressing against the exterior of the shed, locking her and E. together, and she is incapable of thinking, as perhaps she might have thought, and would subsequently think when the ordeal was over, that God was punishing her for leaving the park, the family picnic, without informing her parents . . . that God had detached Himself from her at approximately the moment when she climbed over the stone wall, and began her careless slipping-sliding descent to the road where Edith, or Ethel, awaited her, as an instrument of God's will, pedaling her bicycle on a slow hot dusty August afternoon, a Sunday, and lonely, and nothing to do. As such moments, such decussations in time, like black stitches in familiar flesh, not only determine but define our lives to ourselves . . . but only in retrospect.

For finally of course E. released her. After fifteen minutes, or twenty. And the initial childish relief of it was, N. hadn't wet her pants; hadn't lost control of her bladder; for which she knew the older girl would have taunted her mercilessly, alluded to perpetually, with moronic sniggering persistence, all the years to come of their being classmates, but now suddenly, for no evident reason, it was over, E. unlatched the door, "Okay get the hell out, you, get running little doggie, *you*," E. cried clapping her hands, and N. ran, N. ran as if crazed, out the driveway and to the gravel road and to the hill below the park, aware of yet too dazed to comprehend that the sunshine, the trees, the grass, the very smell of the air, were unchanged, *that nothing had changed,* and climbing the hill sobbing her breath was barbed wire being drawn in, yanked out, of her chest, her throat, her mouth, she was a frenzied little animal unmindful of the thorns and branches that tore at her face, and then, at last, she was nearing the picnic grove, she could smell burning charcoal, she could smell meat, grease, could hear voices, peering over the wall at her family not far away, oblivious of her it seemed, and there were others, other families, in the grove, at picnic tables, at the squat stone fireplaces, young parents like her own and like her Aunt Betty and Uncle Dan, with young children, and there was only, now, that space for her to cross, to be returned to them.

Visitation Rights

I know how to hurt you, the man who was once her husband says.

Not in words of course—he's too clever for that, and too professional—but by way of his silence. By way of his small measured curling smile. By way of the child who is her son five days a week and his son two days a week: forty-eight absolutely precise and clocked hours.

The child's name is Seth and Seth is much loved of course. A five-year-old with the warm shrinking eyes and tentative smile of the much-loved, the fiercely and jealously loved, for there are kisses that have stung his tender skin like the kisses of bees, there are bear hugs that have squeezed the breath out of him, Mommy is herself guilty of having spilled acid-hot tears on his uplifted face and she knows that the man who was once her husband has done worse. She knows.

The man who was once her husband is Seth's father and will always be, so long as he lives, and he means to live a very long time, his father, and he knows his rights, he has been trained in the law (though he dropped out in his second year) and he knows his rights, every inch. Two can play at this game as easily as one he has warned her, and this in actual words, though when she stared at him smiling her small frozen smile he had not repeated the words and afterward, bathing Seth whom she loves more than her life, burying her face in the child's warm neck, she came to doubt she had heard them at all. Since it isn't really like him is it, her parents and her friends and even his friends would find it difficult to believe, it really *isn't* like him is it?—the man who was once her husband and remains her son's father and has custody of him for forty-eight precise and clocked hours a week.

At first it was the movies Seth's father took him to see to which Mommy objected, not movies for five-year-olds she'd have said if she had been consulted as naturally, now, she was not, and never would be again; and the kinds of television programs they watched; and the VCR rentals Seth was patchy in remembering. And for some time— how many weeks or even months Mommy could not determine—a woman had been with them, a woman had helped to dress Seth, and talked to and fussed over and fed breakfast to Seth, a woman faceless, ageless, bodiless, to whom Seth alluded only vaguely and it seemed to Mommy reluctantly, as if he shared in the adults' guilt. "What is her name?" she asked Seth, and Seth said, "I don't know," and she said, "But of course you know—her first name at least," and Seth said, not looking at her, "I don't *know,*" and she resolved not to interrogate him in any serious or protracted way, not even to question him lightly and casually, as if it seemed to her (which in a way it does) a kind of joke; since she isn't a jealous woman and does not intend, at this crucial point in her life, to become a jealous woman . . . examining her son like a police matron inspecting a molested or battered child, gazing into his averted eyes, sniffing his hair and clothing for traces of another woman. "If you don't remember then you don't remember," she said, kissing him. And Seth said gravely, "Yes Mommy."

But she did object to the movies, and the rest of it, and made her objections known to her former husband, not over the telephone (for it was wisest for them, even a year after the divorce, not to speak about anything face to face or over the telephone that was other than a neutral, factual matter) but on a sheet of stationery, neatly typed, and photostatted in duplicate for her and her attorney's files. It particularly enraged her that her son, returned to her on Sunday evenings, was usually, still, in an excitable mood, stubborn about going to bed at his usual time, running wild, making rude noises with his lips—her darling Seth!—and pounding furniture with his fists, his small face flushed as if with fever and his eyes behind their corrective lenses blackly dilated. When she tried to catch him he eluded her, giggling, and butting with his head, and she thought, sick with worry and dread, and a knot of rage throbbing in her heart, This isn't Seth, what is he doing to Seth! How can he be stopped!

So she made her formal objections. And though the man who had once been her husband did not reply the focus of the weekends shifted, as far as she could gauge. There were, now, excursions to the zoo, afternoons at the miniature golf course, educational documentaries on public television, visits to the county museum of natural history—to which, as a child, Mommy herself had been taken. She did not much like the kinds of food her former husband fed her son, nor the restaurants to which, weekend after weekend, he took him, though these—McDonald's, Pizza Hut, International House of Pancakes—were Seth's favorites, as they were the favorites of Seth's classmates and friends, and she did not want to object, and in any case she took hope that, since the other woman was never now alluded to by her son that there was now no woman and perhaps (assuming she had imagined the faint lingering odor of perfume and cigarettes on her son) there had never been one.

And this was entirely possible, even plausible, for hadn't her former husband told her during those final bitter days when they'd still been living together, and free at last to say the many things that had gone unsaid for nearly nine years, hadn't he told her with a strange elated smile that he wanted never to be involved with another woman again? And she'd said, "Good." She'd said, "Good, then you won't ruin another woman's life."

Though secretly she believed that her life, seemingly in a shambles, like the closets and bureau drawers they were going through, was not ruined; not at all ruined; injured perhaps, and surely stunted, but only temporarily. There had been a diapause, and that was all. As soon as the man who had been her husband departed and left her and Seth alone they would both forget him, and be healed of him. So she said quietly, trembling with hatred of him, "Good."

Now there is the zoo, to which she cannot object. The aquarium: dolphins, seals, killer whales. A rodeo at the state capital, a sports car rally, a traveling carnival—though Seth by his own confession stuffed himself on hotdogs and cotton candy, and was sick to his stomach after riding the roller coaster several times in a row. But it is the museum of natural history to which, Saturday following Saturday, her former husband takes her son. And Mommy is relieved; and eager to hear his accounts afterward. It pleases her to envision Seth walking through the very rooms, the very exhibits, through which, years ago, she herself had walked . . . staring in respectful silence at the mannequins of Indians embalmed behind glass (Iroquois, Mohawks), and at a display of the solar system (the planets, singed with dust like age, in perpetual clockwork orbit around the sun); contemplating the prehistoric giants whose bones she'd believed must be real (the skeleton of the great Brontosaurus, the grinning skull of Tyrannosaurus rex, Pterodactyl with bat's wings spread and skinny legs dangling in flight). The very soul of the antiquated building sweeps over her in a flood of memory: the long drafty corridors with their badly worn linoleum tile, the baroque plaster constellations of the distant ceilings, the clanking, grudging radiators. The women's restroom with its disinfectant sour smell.

What had the museum of natural history been to her, as a child, but a kind of godhead: a capacious and seemingly unbounded structure in which numerous deities, delimited and foreshortened as human beings, displayed themselves, innocently brazen, each claiming a portion—but only a portion—of the godhead. Though a place to which children, often in groups, were routinely taken, the museum was not a place for children. Its secrets were too adult.

Millions of butterflies migrating up from South America . . . herds
of Alaskan elk being hunted by Eskimos and timber wolves . . . the
depths of the Pacific Ocean glittering with coral reef, and every
species of fish and sea creature preying on one another . . . a replica-
tion of a prehistoric tar pit in which dinosaurs, flying reptiles, and
enormous birds sank, struggled, died. Once there is even a filmed
laboratory dissection of a human cadaver, a drowned man Seth says,
done at the Johns Hopkins Medical School; there are documentaries
meant to be amusing on the courtship rituals of apes, peacocks,
bumblebees, anacondas. Week following week Seth chatters about
what he has learned, what he is learning, sharing with his father, by
way of the documentary film series at the museum of natural history.
To which she cannot reasonably object.

And then, Sunday evenings, Seth comes home to her, and cannot
settle down. Splashes in the bathtub, unruly, defiant, his skin hot to
the touch and his eyes, without their glasses, damp, myopic, enlarged
. . . beautiful. Mommy's heart is pierced by their beauty, and by their
evasiveness. So cunning has this five-year-old become, he rarely now
refers to his father directly, and never calls him (at least to her)
Daddy; but she can detect the man's voice in his, the subtle nuances
of the man's speech in his, this happy babble of the sunlit African
veldt where herds of gazelle, giraffe, water buffalo are stalked by lions
. . . where packs of dingoes tear the living flesh from stampeding deer
. . . where the sky is black with scavenger birds, and the earth teems
with beetles.

Seth tells Mommy of a clan of monkeys, spider monkeys with long
curling tails, thousands and thousands of spider monkeys he says, and
a lot of baby monkeys with their mothers, he says, and his voice trails
off in silence and she says, with the quick casualness that has become
instinctive in her, "Yes? And what? What about the monkeys?" and
Seth hesitates, and says, "Oh—that was all, Mommy. That was all
there was."

Two Doors

There was a man, who, as a boy, twelve years of age, possibly thirteen, was visiting a cousin's house one summer afternoon, for some reason subsequently forgotten walking upstairs, unaccompanied, along a corridor at the far end of which there was a small roofless porch, a kind of balcony, onto which French doors with latticed windows opened, and midway there he heard a woman's startled cry—not a cry so much as an exclamation of surprise, or annoyance, or simple fear—and he turned to see, in the blurred instant in which a door was closed, in fact slammed, against him, the woman who was his aunt, his young aunt, his mother's younger sister, only partly clothed, in something white, and filmy, edged with lace, showing her warm bare shoulders and the pale tops of her breasts, her long pale arms, and her legs and feet too appeared to be bare, or so, in that confused fleeting moment, it seemed, for he had no more than a glance, a glimpse, his eyes narrowing instinctively as if something—a baseball, a bird—were hurtling itself at him; and then he was past and the door was shut and momentum carried him to wherever he was going, and no mention was made that day or any other day of the door slammed against his innocent staring eyes nor did he apologize to his aunt for his intrusion, his blunder, a misstep like stumbling on a flight of stairs in a dream and waking himself from sleep, heart pounding and senses alert . . . which happened, frequently, in those years.

And through his adolescence and young adulthood he was haunted
by, it might almost be said at times obsessed with, the memory of the
slammed door; the glimpse of a woman, faceless, only partly clothed,
slamming the door against him—against *him!*—and he meant no
harm!—though the actual woman, his mother's sister, aging, was of
virtually no interest to him, as his twelve-year-old self, long displaced,
dead, was of no interest to him. And then he was in love, and then
he married, and then he had children, and life accelerated, as we
outlive, not ourselves, but our succession of selves, and the memory
receded, and if he dreamt it was likely to be of Tibetan mountains
rising out of mists, which, apart from photographs, he had never seen,
or crimson and green plumed birds of the Amazonian rain forest,
with jeweled eyes, which, in pastel crayons, he tried clumsily to
sketch, and there were geometrical figures which haunted him to no
purpose, and elusive strains of music that did not resolve themselves
into melodies, and he fell in love not with women any longer but with
tones . . . textures . . . qualities of light . . . with snowfall, with the
dwarf irises in his garden, with the steepled horizon seen from a hotel
window in Tangier, where he traveled, alone and bereft, after his
wife's death. And the old memory would have been extinguished
altogether . . . except, now, tonight, he is forcibly reminded, passing
by an upstairs room in this house in which he finds himself living, a
sort of permanent guest, and a door is quickly, quietly shut against
him, is it his granddaughter's room?—that girl, tall, slender, with
perfectly straight pale hair and cloudless eyes that, moving onto him,
move as fluidly off?—as if his death already inhabited him, and the
very space in which he stands is vacant. And this time, outraged, he
closes his fingers about the doorknob, to open it, to confront and to
accuse, to explain.

Desire

All his life he has been lonely so naturally he marries often. Impregnates the women as quickly as possible then stands back, observing, to wait.

He loves the fat swelling bellies, the beautiful women staggering with their own weight as if deliciously drunk—that grip of a woman's fingers on his arm, the warm moist breath. He loves the heavy breasts filled to bursting, giving suck to drowsy babies, leaking milk on the pillow. He loves even the knowing that these lives depend so utterly upon *his.*

So he tells himself: I love.

Actually he gets bored fairly quickly. He tries for constancy, fidelity, the old honored virtues, but it doesn't work: that isn't his nature. A pang of desire strikes keen and sharp as a wire piercing his flesh and he knows he must move on and, well, he does move on . . . these matters can't be legislated after all.

The heart has its reasons, says Pascal. That reason knows not.

Or words to that effect.

All his life he has been lonely so naturally he seeks friendship . . . friends. Boys in school, men in his profession, the husbands of his wives' friends, and in some cases the husbands of the women with whom he sleeps. Hello he says and shakes hands and his frank staring eyes seek out the other's in a plea that is sometimes (he knows, to his shame) too direct, too raw. At other times it is all under control and the conversation springs up naturally, the swift happy coincidences of certain hobbies, sports, political beliefs, hopes. When he gets to know a man reasonably well and is certain the man will not betray him by violating his confidence he might tell him as if casually about his loneliness; his *mysterious* loneliness. (Is it shared? Is it even understood?) He has perhaps too frequently and too impulsively confessed that he'd always envied children with large families—older sisters, brothers—he'd observed them out of his particular aloneness as the only child of "older" parents and believed that, there, amid even the bickering and pummeling, *there* lay the secret of all happiness.

Only once, misinterpreting a friend's sympathy as an invitation to further intimacy, did he dare ask the man about *his* present circumstances. Was he happily married?—was he happy, being a father? Or did he too, from time to time, feel this strange inexplicable all-pervading loneliness?—the mere word inadequate to describe an emptiness ten times emptied, a void, a nullity, a vacuum from which all light, color, texture, substance, form have fled?

His friend looked at him sharply and he saw that the man was no friend. The answer came swiftly: Yes. Of course he was happy. Of course from time to time he felt "lonely"—briefly—who doesn't? But why is it important?

He thinks: How much harder to court another man, than any woman. How much more treacherous—dangerous. To a woman you can say, Shall we make love? Shall we get married? But to no man can you say, Shall we be friends? Shall we be—*brothers*?

For it's really a brother he wants, not a friend. Not a sister—his childhood fantasies never really involved sisters—just a brother! a single brother! And his life, so unsatisfying, so curiously lacerated, would have been whole.

There was a pretty young woman, one of his wives in fact, who chided him often for being so "morbid." For thinking about the kinds of things other people rarely thought about.

"Meaning—?"

"I don't know. Death, dying, that sort of thing. The purpose behind things, or what people do," she said carelessly. "I don't know. But I don't like it."

He asked the young woman pleasantly what were the things she believed he should think about, in that case.

"Me. Us. The baby."

"Well—of course I do."

"Do you?"

"I do."

"Yes but *do* you?"

He was beginning not to be charmed but he laughed and kissed her, for all things, with women, with *his* women, were resolved in kisses until such time as his desire died.

But he thought, She knows.

He thought, I haven't deceived this one.

What it was, however, that the young woman knew, and knew about him, he could not have named.

He blames his parents, he *was* an only child.

He blames his parents, they had him so very late it was almost *too* late.

A mother forty years older than he and a father fifty-two years older . . . He loved them but they weren't enough, not nearly enough, there was his white-haired father laughing when asked if the little boy was his grandchild, "No, he happens to be my son," while his mother stood stiff and indignant and said nothing at all.

There was the quiet house, the still house, the house that in his memory, is empty; waiting to be filled.

It isn't true of course that he blames his parents, he knows better. He's a reasonable man, an adult, no longer a child pining away in loneliness. He's a man with a "solid reputation" in his profession and he's a "success" you might say (he grants himself a moderate success, at least). And if he falls in love often, and marries often, and has fathered too many children, it's out of an excess of feeling, an extravagant spiritual generosity—you might say.

"You're the most romantic man I know," a woman once told him. "You seem to have such faith."

"I do? Do I?" he'd asked excitedly. "Faith in what, do you think—?"

He begins to read voraciously in his spare time. And not always in his spare time, but at his desk, in secret, when he really ought to be attending to other things. Gilt-stamped luxury volumes of simulated leather smelling of newness, and antiquity—the "wisdom of the ages" from Plato to Wittgenstein. Or handsome paperback editions of classics that, in his time, were scorned by his generation as no longer relevant to theirs. Dickens, Swift, Shakespeare—of course—but it is Milton who most engages his imagination; and these lines from *Paradise Lost* that arouse in him a sympathy so intense he understands it is one of the secrets of his emotional life.

> *I thither went*
> *With unexperienc't thought, and laid me down*
> *On the green bank, to look into the clear*
> *Smooth Lake, that to me seem'd another Sky.*
> *As I bent down to look, just opposite,*
> *A Shape within the wat'ry gleam appear'd*
> *Bending to look on me, I started back,*

It started back, but pleas'd I soon return'd,
Pleas'd it return'd as soon with answering looks
Of sympathy and love; and there I had fixt
Mine eyes till now, and pin'd with vain desire.

———————◆———————

By the time he is fifty-seven years old he has married four times, is
responsible for the financial upkeep of several households, yet he falls
in love again—again!—and marries again, a woman already pregnant
with his child. When the baby is born this will be how many children?—six? seven? And his young wife will very likely want another.

"I'm greedy," she says. "Like you."

And then one day he learns that he has a tumorous growth in his
colon that must be removed; and is removed; and is discovered to be
benign. But during the course of the operation the surgeon discovers
another growth in his lower abdomen—the mummified remains,
weighing scarcely an ounce, of what was to have been his twin.

His twin!

Such things happen, sometimes, his doctor tells him. Of course it's
highly unusual—monozygotic or "identical" twins are in themselves
highly unusual—and in these rare cases it happens that one fetus
drains blood and oxygen from the other and gradually overpowers it,
kills it, absorbs it into his body. And at the time of his birth, long
before today's medical technology, no one knew, of course, that there
had ever been another fetus in his mother's womb.

"Then I was meant to have a twin?—to be a twin?" he asks,
astonished.

"Evidently not," says his doctor. "Considering the evidence."

Smiling he weighs the thing in the palm of his hand.

He contemplates it, pokes it with a finger: tough little calcified
rubber knob, a wizened plum, just—nothing. You'd never guess what

it is or from where it was taken and you'd never be able to tell from looking at it, peering at it under the desk lamp, whether it's something to laugh over, or mourn. Sometimes, staring at it, he can't control his laughter—tears streak his face. His twin! His! Fifty-seven years later! Other times, he's mute with grief. Sits unmoving just staring transfixed at the thing in the palm of his hand that, weightless, weighs so much.

"So this is it," he says.

His wife says, "You wouldn't be so unhappy if you thought about other people for a change, instead of always—whatever it is, you think about."

He says pleasantly, "What *is* it, do you imagine, that I think about?—that I shouldn't, I mean, think about."

"I don't know," she says evenly. "I don't know but I don't like it. It's just something I sense."

She's twenty-six years younger than he and knows she will outlive him. Or walk away from him when it's time—the first of his wives to do so.

Carefully he asks, "What should I think about, then?"

"Me. Us. The new baby. Your other children."

"But I do. I think about you all the time."

"Do you?" she asks skeptically.

"Of course," he says smiling. "What else is there, after all, to think about?"

Train

Walking alone . . . seems to be following a stranger, a young woman, it's an urban setting but not this city, no city he knows or can recollect, deserted streets and sidewalks and a light rain falling, the smell of mist, cold, that piercing healing smell, and the woman knows he's following her and begins to walk faster her heels clattering against the pavement but suddenly she has turned to confront him: I don't know you do I. We aren't acquainted are we. Please leave me alone. I won't tell anyone if you leave me alone if you let me walk away and don't follow me, speaking calmly but of course he isn't deceived, —if you let me walk away and don't follow me. And sometimes out of the magnitude of pity, he does.

. . . His reflected face in the window close by. Night pressed up against the glass and no distracting lights only the cloud-massed sky that has an inky oily look tonight but when he gets to his feet he'll see lights burning below in the building across the street which is ten floors high while the building in which he works is eighteen floors high and his office is on the eighteenth now meaning he is at the top or as far in any case as he's likely to go and it *is* far, *has* been far, he's properly grateful of course. It might be said (has been said?) that the promise he once represented in the eyes of his elders has been generously fulfilled as one by one they have eased aside to make way for him—retiring, dying, disappearing in turn though not without having conferred their blessings on him otherwise he wouldn't be in this sumptuous corner office, desk long and wide as a coffin, and as polished. Would not have his secretary who in turn has a trio of young-girl assistants. Would not work here on the eighteenth floor with a view of infinity.

Recall William of Occam . . . *never to multiply entities beyond simplicity.*

Black-tie says the invitation. So he wears his tuxedo, gold studs, his wife wears a black cocktail dress, taffeta skirt and gauze overskirt, stockings with a smart startling blackish sheen. Three hundred dollars a couple and it's for a good cause like all such causes: nuclear arms control: salmon steak, grilled, and rather dry; potatoes carved to resemble something other than potatoes; specialty salad greens, excellent imported wines. Flashbulbs and TV cameras and the celebrity speaker speaks impassioned of nuclear winter the extinction of the (human) species and he's emptying one of the wine bottles into his glass hurrying to catch the train which is a train both like and unlike the commuter train he takes twice daily the same slightly soiled plush high-backed seats the same armrests and litter underfoot but the lighting seems different something about the ceiling is different and the shape of the windows and he has his choice of seats which is unusual so he sits in one then changes his mind and switches to another across the aisle and there's his face reflected in the window awaiting him but he changes his mind again (the seat is sticky, there's a disagreeable smell of pipe tobacco, perhaps there *is* someone sitting just in front of him and he'd rather be alone) so he carries his briefcase into the next car and again the car is nearly empty except for a woman

seated to his left, a young woman whose face he can't see but he has
the idea she is someone he knows or someone who knows him, he
leans over the seat asks if the seat is taken and she glances up startled
just perceptibly frightened but shakes her head no, the seat isn't
taken. So he sits down.

... Noticing that his clothes don't quite fit, in the old way. He's doing
things with his left hand more frequently. *The whorl of his hair resists
the comb.* Every year the weight of it, sweetish ashes in the mouth
... November shading into December and the days rudely truncated
as the heartbeat accelerates to keep pace. Waking from dreams exhausted lying without moving neither asleep nor awake recalling a
marriage, "his," but to whom, and why, though the woman sleeps
beside him that deep trusting flesh-heavy sleep of years. Should he
feel "something is wrong" not seriously wrong of course but mildly
wrong, an ache in his eyes, that sense of the floor's subtle tilt, the
withheld smile of a friend when he'd naturally expected a warmer
greeting. Something *is* wrong and it makes him angry. Makes him
damned angry his heartbeat quick and hard and on the edge of
hurting. Thinking of old betrayals, injuries, insults lacerating the soul
but received stoically at the time . . . because he hadn't quite understood their significance or because he'd been stupid or because he'd
been generous-minded as one hopes to be throughout a life and
there's day shifting to dusk and to night without your noticing and
suddenly that reflection in the plate-glass window floating in space,
again, watching. Patient holes for eyes, watching.

A length of twine in his pocket. Why twine you ask but why *not.* And
consider: the clumsy bulk of a knife, the embarrassment of an actual
knife. Whereas *twine*—it's for wrapping packages isn't it. This is
special twine wire-reinforced impossible to break by hand and virtually impossible to cut except with a shears manipulated by strong
fingers.

Does it have anything to do with me   anything to do with us   is
it something at work   are you tired   are you ill   are you
worried about something   can't you tell me   please tell me and
he says no more sharply than he intends dreading her touch her
look of hurt and fear and reproach then repenting, more gently, says,
—I mean no, it's nothing.

(Embracing her, his face hidden in her hair. *No.*)

. . . One of the walls is glass looking out upon trees in staggered
profusion and at dusk there too reflections define themselves shyly at
first, indistinct as reflections in a well. The interior of the long living
room, the fireplace, familiar lamps and their haloes of light you could
call warm, domestic. A man stands staring motionless, staring. These
interior images begin to push back the dissolving trees and shrubs
beyond the glass and if he steps forward into them he will find himself
in a place smelling of damp, of earth and leaf and mold, a stinging
in his eyes but the impact of the fresh freezing air is good, filling his
lungs as he begins to run as he hasn't run in years running swiftly
downhill his arms pumping and his heels sinking into the earth his
breath coming too quickly and harshly but God! the air! this dark
bright air! running, flying, plunging—plunging.

Telephones his wife . . . to explain he will be having dinner with a
client, last-minute alteration of plans and she's silent for a moment
as if knowing (but how can she know) he is lying (but *is* he lying)
and he's in the men's room shaving for the second time that day
though more carefully now, ceremonially, not his face but the face,
the one she'll see. Changes his shirt, knots a new tie around his neck,
small simple pleasures that reaffirm one's place in the world of shirts,
ties, suits, polished shoes. Whorl of the hair resists the comb . . . in
the old way. But this is new feeling invigorated, excited, refreshed as

if he'd just woken from sleep and it's 7:50, he's one of the last to leave the building as usual and the black janitor humming to himself with mop and pail casts him an ambiguous look and calls out g'night Mr. —— and he calls out in turn good night and is about to add the man's name but thinks better of it, doesn't want to seem condescending. The janitor says jovially but inscrutably doan look like a bad night out there and he says well—that's good. Pushing out the heavy glass door into the lightly falling snow clean as artificial white chips falling languidly in a glass paperweight and he's wondering if he and the black janitor have had this exchange many times before and will they have it again or will tonight be the final time.

(The suburban ranch house they'd rented when they were first married where the previous tenants had kept white mice, ferrets, tropical fish, and before moving out they'd killed them all and buried them in the backyard and by accident he discovered the bodies partly decomposed in a shallow slovenly grave just a few shovelfuls of sandy soil and rubbish . . . saying to her don't look it's nothing, don't look. And she didn't.)

. . . Saying quietly, I think you do know me. She says, no. He says, yes I'm sure you do. She's a tall young woman though not as tall as he. Fleshy, a smooth fine skin, not beautiful but attractive enough and she's licking her lower lip nervously, I'm afraid not, she says, she's hesitating not wanting to break it off too quickly yet there's something not quite right she's thinking and he says still quietly, Why don't we talk it over, where can we have a drink, he's speaking slowly and calmly and she hesitates and he doesn't say anything further just allows her to decide: Well—O.K.

The 11:40 train which he hasn't taken in a very long time, some of the cars entirely empty, the high-backed shabby seats, sticky floors, windows shiny with grease and he's walking hurriedly along the aisle rejecting each seat as he passes, if only he could find someone he knows to sit beside or someone who knows him or the idea of him, a neighbor preferably, a friend of his and his wife's preferably, but there are few passengers at this time of night and the train is moving and he's frantic looking while trying not to appear frantic peering at faces until in the fifth car—or in the sixth, or seventh—a man glances up at him from a folded newspaper as he approaches swaying with the train's drunken motion and their eyes lock and yes it's someone who seems to know him—though he can't recall the man's name and they won't introduce themselves but he sits with him his chest heaving in agitation and relief and the pain there subsiding as they're being borne out of the city companionable and silent into and through and out of the long tunnel into the suburban countryside to the north where each has his home.

The Others

Early one evening in a crowd of people, most of them commuters, he happened to see, quite by accident—he'd taken a slightly different route that day, having left the building in which he worked by an entrance he rarely used—and this, as he'd recall afterward, with the fussy precision which had characterized him since childhood, and helped to account for his success in his profession, because there was renovation being done in the main lobby—a man he had not seen in years, or was it decades: a face teasingly familiar, yet made strange by time, like an old photograph about to disintegrate into its elements.

Spence followed the man into the street, into a blowsy damp dusk, but did not catch up to him and introduce himself: that wasn't his way. He was certain he knew the man, and that the man knew him, but how, or why, or from what period in his life the man dated, he could not have said. Spence was forty-two years old and the other seemed to be about that age, yet, oddly, older: his skin liverish, his profile vague as if seen through an element transparent yet dense, like water; his clothing—handsome tweed overcoat, sharply creased gray trousers—hanging slack on him, as if several sizes too large.

Outside, Spence soon lost sight of the man in a swarm of pedestrians crossing the street; and made no effort to locate him again. But for most of the ride home on the train he thought of nothing else: who was that man, why was he certain the man would have known him, what were they to each other, resembling each other only very slightly, yet close as twins? He felt stabs of excitement that left him weak and breathless but it wasn't until that night, when he and his wife were undressing for bed, that he said, or heard himself say, in a voice of bemused wonder, and dread: "I saw someone today who looked just like my cousin Sandy—"

"Did I know Sandy?" his wife asked.

"—my cousin Sandy who died, who drowned, when we were both in college."

"But did I know him?" his wife asked. She cast him an impatient sidelong glance and smiled her sweet-derisive smile. "It's difficult to envision him if I've never seen him, and if he's been dead for so long, why should it matter so much to you?"

Spence had begun to perspire. His heart beat hard and steady as if in the presence of danger. "I don't understand what you're saying," he said.

"The actual words, or their meaning?"

"The words."

She laughed as if he had said something witty, and did not answer him. As he fell asleep he tried not to think of his cousin Sandy whom he had not seen in twenty years and whom he'd last seen in an open casket in a funeral home in Damascus, Minnesota.

The second episode occurred a few weeks later when Spence was in line at a post office, not the post office he usually frequented but another, larger, busier, in a suburban township adjacent to his own, and the elderly woman in front of him drew his attention: wasn't she, too, someone he knew? or had known, many years ago? He stared, fascinated, at her stitched-looking skin, soft and puckered as a glove of some exquisite material, and unnaturally white; her eyes that were small, sunken, yet shining; her astonishing hands—delicate, even skeletal, discolored by liver spots like coins, yet with rings on several fingers, and in a way rather beautiful. The woman appeared to be in her mid-nineties, if not older: fussy, anxious, very possibly addled: complaining ceaselessly to herself, or to others by way of herself. Yet her manner was mirthful; nervous bustling energy crackled about her like invisible bees.

He believed he knew who she was: Miss Reuter, a teacher of his in elementary school. Whom he had not seen in more years than he wanted to calculate.

Miss Reuter, though enormously aged, was able, it seemed, to get around by herself. She carried a large rather glitzy shopping bag made of a silvery material, and in this bag, and in another at her feet, she was rummaging for her change purse, as she called it, which she could not seem to find. The post office clerk waited with a show of strained patience; the line now consisted of a half-dozen people.

Spence asked Miss Reuter—for surely it was she: while virtually unrecognizable she was at the same time unmistakable—if she needed some assistance. He did not call her by name and as she turned to him, in exasperation, and gratitude—as if she knew that he, or someone, would come shortly to her aid—she did not seem to recognize him. Spence paid for her postage and a roll of stamps and Miss Reuter, still rummaging in her bag, vexed, cheerful, befuddled, thanked him without looking up at him. She insisted it must be a loan, and not a gift, for she was, she said, "not yet an object of public charity."

Afterward Spence put the incident out of his mind, knowing the woman was dead. It was purposeless to think of it, and would only upset him.

After that he began to see them more frequently. The Others, —as he thought of them. On the street, in restaurants, at church; in the building in which he worked; on the very floor, in the very department, in which his office was located. (He was a tax lawyer for one

of the largest of American "conglomerates"—yes and very well paid.)
One morning his wife saw him standing at a bedroom window look-
ing out toward the street. She poked him playfully in the ribs.
"What's wrong?" she said. "None of this behavior suits you."

"There's someone out there, at the curb."

"No one's there."

"I have the idea he's waiting for me."

"Oh yes, I do see someone," his wife said carelessly. "He's often
there. But I doubt that he's waiting for you."

She laughed, as at a private joke. She was a pretty freckled snub-
nosed woman given to moments of mysterious amusement. Spence
had married her long ago in a trance of love from which he had yet
to awaken.

Spence said, his voice shaking, "I think—I'm afraid I think I might
be having a nervous breakdown. I'm so very, very afraid."

"No," said his wife, "—you're the sanest person I know. All surface and no cracks, fissures, potholes."

Spence turned to her. His eyes were filling with tears.

"Don't joke. Have pity."

She made no reply; seemed about to drift away; then slipped an
arm around his waist and nudged her head against his shoulder in a
gesture of camaraderie. Whether mocking, or altogether genuine,
Spence could not have said.

"It's just that I'm so afraid."

"Yes, you've said."

"—of losing my mind. Going mad."

She stood for a moment, peering out toward the street. The elderly
gentleman standing at the curb glanced back but could not have seen
them, or anyone, behind the lacy bedroom curtains. He was well
dressed, and carried an umbrella. An umbrella? Perhaps it was a
cane.

Spence said, "I seem to be seeing, more and more, these people—
people I don't think are truly there."

"*He's* there."

"I think they're dead. Dead people."

His wife drew back and cast him a sidelong glance, smiling mysteriously. "It does seem to have upset you," she said.

"Since I know they're not there—"

"He's there,"

"—so I must be losing my mind. A kind of schizophrenia, waking dreams, hallucinations—"

Spence was speaking excitedly, and did not know exactly what he was saying. His wife drew away from him in alarm, or distaste.

"You take everything so personally," she said.

One morning shortly after the New Year, when the air was sharp as a knife, and the sky so blue it brought tears of pain to one's eyes, Spence set off on the underground route from his train station to his building. Beneath the city's paved surface was a honeycomb of tunnels, some of them damp and befouled but most of them in good condition, with, occasionally, a corridor of gleaming white tiles that looked as if it had been lovingly polished by hand. Spence preferred aboveground, or believed he should prefer aboveground, for reasons vague and puritanical, but in fierce weather he made his way underground, and worried only that he might get lost, as he sometimes did. (Yet, even lost, he had only to find an escalator or steps leading to the street—and he was no longer lost.)

This morning, however, the tunnels were far more crowded than usual. Spence saw a preponderance of elderly men and women, with here and there a young face, startling, and seemingly unnatural. Here and there, yet more startling, a child's face. Very few of the faces had that air, so disconcerting to him in the past, of the eerily familiar laid upon the utterly unfamiliar; and these he resolutely ignored.

He soon fell into step with the crowd, keeping to their pace—which was erratic, surging, faster along straight stretches of tunnel and slower at curves; he found it agreeable to be borne along by the flow, as of a tide. A tunnel of familiar tear-stained mosaics yielded to one of the smart gleaming tunnels and that in turn to a tunnel badly in need of repair—and, indeed, being noisily repaired, by one of those crews of workmen that labor at all hours of the day and night beneath the surface of the city—and as Spence hurried past the deafening vibrations of the air hammer he found himself descending stairs into a tunnel unknown to him: a place of warm, humming, droning sound, like conversation, though none of his fellow pedestrians seemed to be talking. Where were they going, so many people? And in the same direction?—with only, here and there, a lone, clearly lost individual bucking the tide, white-faced, eyes snatching at his as if in desperate recognition.

Might as well accompany them, Spence thought, and see.

Blue-Bearded Lover

I.

When we walked together he held my hand unnaturally high, at the level of his chest, as no man had done before. In this way he made his claim.

When we stood at night beneath the great winking sky he instructed me gently in its deceit. The stars you see above you, he said, have vanished thousands of millions of years ago; it is precisely the stars you cannot see that exist, and exert their influence upon you.

When we lay together in the tall cold grasses the grasses curled lightly over us as if to hide us.

II.

A man's passion is his triumph, I have learned. And to be the receptacle of a man's passion is a woman's triumph.

III.

He made me his bride and brought me to his great house which smelled of time and death. Passageways and doors and high-ceilinged rooms and tall windows opening out onto nothing. Have you ever loved another man as you now love me? my blue-bearded lover asked. Do you give your life to me?

What is a woman's life that cannot be thrown away!

He told me of the doors I may unlock and the rooms I may enter freely. He told me of the seventh door, the forbidden door, which I may not unlock: for behind it lies a forbidden room which I may not enter. Why may I not enter it? I asked, for I saw that he expected it of me, and he said, kissing my brow, Because I have forbidden it.

And he entrusted me with the key to the door, for he was going away on a long journey.

IV.

Here it is: a small golden key, weighing no more than a feather in the palm of my hand.

It is faintly stained as if with blood. It glistens when I hold it to the light.

Did I not know that my lover's previous brides had been brought to this house to die?—that they had failed him, one by one, and had deserved their fate?

I have slipped the golden key into my bosom, to wear against my heart, as a token of my lover's trust in me.

V.

When my blue-bearded lover returned from his long journey he was gratified to see that the door to the forbidden room remained locked; and when he examined the key, still warm from my bosom, he saw that the stain was an old, old stain, and not of my doing.

And he declared with great passion that I was now truly his wife; and that he loved me above all women.

VI.

Through the opened windows the invisible stars exert their power.
But if it is a power that is known, are the stars invisible?

When I sleep in our sumptuous bed I sleep deeply, and dream
dreams that I cannot remember afterward, of extraordinary beauty,
I think, and magic, and wonder. Sometimes in the morning my
husband will recall them for me, for their marvels are such they
invade even his dreams. How is it that you of all persons can dream
such dreams, he says, —such curious works of art!

And he kisses me, and seems to forgive me.

And I will be bearing his child soon. The first of his many children.

Secret Observations on the Goat-Girl

At the edge of my father's property, in an abandoned corncrib, there lives a strange creature—a goat-child—a girl—my age—with no name that we know—and no mother or father or companions. She has a long narrow head and immense slanted eyes, albino-pale, and an expression that seems to be perpetually startled. The veins of her eyes glow a faint warm pulsing pink and the irises are animal-slits, vertical, very black. Sometimes she suns herself in the open doorway, her slender front legs tucked neatly beneath her, her head alert and uplifted. Sometimes she grazes in the back pasture. Though we children are forbidden to know about her we frequently spy on her, and laugh to see her down on all fours, *grazing as animals do*—yet in an awkward improvised posture, as if she were a child playing at being a goat.

But of course she *is* an animal and frightening to see.

Her small body is covered in coarse white hairs, wavy, slightly curly, longest around her temples and at the nape of her neck. Her ears are frankly goatish, pert and oversized and sensitive to the slightest sound. (If we creep up in the underbrush to spy on her, she always hears us—her ears prick up and tremble—though she doesn't seem to see us. Which is why some of us have come to believe that the goat-girl is blind.)

Her nose, like her ears, is goatish: snubbed and flat with wide dark nostrils. But her eyes are human eyes. Thickly lashed and beautiful. Except they are so very pale. The tiny blood vessels are exposed which is why they look pink; I wonder, does the sunshine hurt her? . . . do tears form in her eyes? (Of my eight brothers and sisters it is the older, for some reason, who argue that the goat-girl is blind and should be put out of her misery. One of my sisters has nightmares about her—about her strange staring eyes—though she has seen the goat-girl only once, and then from a distance of at least fifteen feet. Oh the nasty thing, she says, half sobbing, the filthy thing!—Father should have it butchered.)

But we all speak in whispers. Because we are forbidden to know.

Since the goat-girl came to live at the edge of our property my mother rarely leaves the house. In fact she rarely comes downstairs now. Sometimes she wears a robe over her nightgown and doesn't brush out her hair and pin it up the way she used to, sometimes she hurries out of the room if one of us comes in. Her laughter is faint and shrill.

Her fingers are cold to the touch. She doesn't embrace us any longer.

Father doesn't admonish her because, as he says, he loves her too deeply. But he often avoids her. And of course he is very busy with his travels—he is sometimes absent for weeks at a time.

Shame, shame!—the villagers whisper.

But never so that any of us can hear.

The goat-girl cannot speak as human beings do, nor does she make goat noises. For the most part she is silent. But she is capable of a strangulated mew, a bleating whine, and, sometimes at night, a questioning cry that is human in its intonation and rhythm, though of course it is incomprehensible, and disturbing to hear. To some of us it sounds pleading, to others angry and accusing. Of course no one ever replies.

The goat-girl eats grass, grain, vegetables the farm workers have tossed into her pen—gnarled and knotted carrots, wormy turnips, blackened potatoes. One day I slipped away from the house to bring her a piece of my birthday cake (angel food with pink frosting and a sprinkling of silver "stars")—I left it wrapped in a napkin near the corncrib but as far as I knew she never approached it: she is very shy by daylight.

(Except when she believes no one is near. Then you should see how delightful she is, playing in the meadow, trotting and frisking about, kicking up her little hooves!—exactly like any young animal, without a worry in the world.)

The goat-girl has no name, just as she has no mother or father. But she is a girl and so it seems cruel to call her *it*. I will baptize her Astrid because the name makes me think of snow and the goat-girl's hair is snowy white.

The years pass and the goat-girl continues to live in the old corncrib at the edge of our property. No one speaks of her—no one wonders at the fact that she has grown very little since she came to live with us. (When I was nine years old I thought the goat-girl was my age exactly and that she would grow along with me, like a sister. But I must have been mistaken.)

Mother no longer comes downstairs at all. It is possible that people have forgotten her in the village. My brothers and sisters and I would forget her too except for her rapid footsteps overhead and her occasional laughter. Sometimes we hear doors being slammed upstairs— my parents' voices—dim and muffled—the words never audible.

Father asks us to pray for Mother. Which of course we have been doing all along.

By night the goat-girl becomes a nocturnal creature and loses her shyness in a way that is surprising. She leaves the safety of her pen, leaves her little pasture, and prowls anywhere she wishes. Sometimes we hear her outside our windows—her cautious hooves in the grass, her low bleating murmur. I wish I could describe the sound she makes!—it is gentle, it is pleading, it is reproachful, it is trembling with rage—a fluid wordless questioning—like music without words—*Why? How long? Who?*—stirring us from sleep.

Now I see that, by moonlight, the goat-girl is terrifying to watch. Many times I have crept from my bed to look down at her, through my gauzy curtains, protected (I believe) by the dark, and have been frightened by her stiff little body, her defiant posture, her glaring pale eyes. I want to cry out—Please don't hate me!—Please don't wish me harm!—but of course I say nothing, not even a whisper. I draw back from the window and tiptoe to my bed and try to sleep and in the morning it might be that the goat-girl appeared to all my brothers and sisters during the night. . . . But I wasn't asleep, I didn't dream, I try to explain, I saw her myself; but they say mockingly, No, no, you were dreaming too, you are no different from the rest of us, it wouldn't dare come this close to the house.

She isn't *it,* I tell them. Her name is Astrid.

Father dreams of her death but is too weak to order it, so my oldest brother plans to arrange for the butchering as soon as he comes to maturity. Until then the goat-girl lives quietly and happily enough at the edge of our property, sunning herself in good weather, browsing in the pasture, frisking and gamboling about. Singing her plaintive little mew to herself. Trespassing by moonlight. One day soon I will creep as close as possible to look into her eyes, to judge if they are human or not, if they are blind.

She has grown very little over the years but her haunches are muscular, her nearly human shoulders, neck, and head are more defined, sometimes I see her child-soul pushing up out of her goat body like a swimmer emerging from a frothy white sea, about to gasp for air, blink and gape in amazement.

Astrid! I will call. Sister!

But she won't know her name.

The Stadium

There was a man, no longer young, though not yet old, who, traveling alone in northern Europe, began to feel that his soul was being drained slowly, almost secretly from him, drop by drop. He woke frequently in the night, in unfamiliar hotel beds, his eyes opened wide and sightless, his damp hair stuck to his forehead. In the northernmost city of his itinerary, where, at the summer solstice, the sun barely set, and the sky was eerily illuminated through the brief night, he knew himself close to oblivion. Why am I not more frightened, he wondered. Much of his life had been passed in a careful, civilized sort of fear, always under control. He had made this fear, and his control of it, more or less his life's work; his art. Yet now, alone, his senses alert to the point of pain, he was scarcely afraid at all. He supposed it had something to do with the unnatural fading of the night.

In the morning he stood shirtless at a window of his hotel room, observing the sky, which was a faint marbled blue, radiant with Arctic cold. He drew a deep breath, and trembled with a sensation very like bliss. Why so happy! he wondered. He felt, in that instant, that all of his life, his true life, still lay before him.

Though, later that morning, he would be obliged to give a lecture at the university, before an audience of several hundred people, and must dress the part, in expensive, custom-made suits—for he was, in his public self, a "distinguished" man—now he put on old clothes, running shoes, a woolen hat, and gloves. He left the hotel, and went to run in an enormous civic stadium that had been pointed out to him the day before by his interpreter. The air was fresh and alien to the taste, blindingly bright, the wind so percussive it took his breath away.

The stadium, built within the past few years, already looked, to his eye, disconcertingly shabby; its walls of poured concrete rain-streaked as if tear-streaked; its walkways narrow, with a pervasive odor of damp, and of something more malevolent, like backed-up drains. Grit-encrusted weeds poked their way, like evil thoughts, through cracks in the pavement. And the size of the stadium, for which he should have been prepared, was really quite . . . disconcerting. Rows of seats, empty seats, lifted above him, and behind him; on all sides; the space was the size of a small city. Approximately half the seats were exposed in the harsh sunshine, and half were obscured in shadow that appeared too dark to be, at this time of day, altogether natural. And the cinder track, which should have been no more than a mile long, stretched nearly out of sight, a foreshortened and distended circle.

He wondered suddenly why he had come to this place; what force had drawn him. But of course it was too late to turn back.

He pulled the woolen cap down low on his forehead, and began to run.

And began to hear, almost at once, at his back, and rising vertiginously overhead, a low, murmurous sound, as of a great crowd. He could feel its collective anticipation, its very nearly palpable excitement; he could hear the humming of the amplifying system; the small black cinders crunched beneath his hard-driving feet with a faint air of protest. The thought came calmly to him, Here are fine-ground bones, preceding yours.

Still, he ran. A small, solitary figure, he ran.

About the Author

Joyce Carol Oates is the author of numerous works of fiction, poetry, criticism, and drama. Her books include, *First Love, George Bellows; American Artist, Where is Here?, I Lock My Door Upon Myself, On Boxing,* and *The Perfectionist and Other Plays,* all available from The Ecco Press. A recipient of the National Book Award and the Rea Award for Achievement in the Short Story, she lives in Princeton, New Jersey, where she is the Roger S. Berlind Distinguished Professor in the Humanities at Princeton University.